OUTSIDE STORIES

Essays by Eliot Weinberger

OUTSIDE STORIES

BY ELIOT WEINBERGER

AUTHOR

Works on Paper (1986)
19 Ways of Looking at Wang Wei (with Octavio Paz, 1987)
Invenciones de papel (tr. P. Jiménez, 1990)
Outside Stories (1992)

EDITOR

Montemora (1975–1982)
Poesía norteamericana desde 1950 (1992)

EDITOR & TRANSLATOR

Octavio Paz, *Eagle or Sun?* (1970; revised edition, 1976)
Octavio Paz, *A Draft of Shadows* (1980)
Homero Aridjis, *Exaltation of Light* (1981)
Octavio Paz, *Selected Poems* (1984)
Jorge Luis Borges, *Seven Nights* (1984)
Octavio Paz, *Collected Poems 1957–1987* (1987)
Vicente Huidobro, *Altazor* (1988)
Octavio Paz, *A Tree Within* (1988)
Octavio Paz, *Sunstone* (1991)
Cecilia Vicuña, *Unravelling Words and the Weaving of Water* (1992)
Xavier Villaurrutia, *Nostalgia for Death* (1992)

Eliot Weinberger

OUTSIDE STORIES

1987–1991

A NEW DIRECTIONS BOOK

Many of these essays first appeared in Mexico in Spanish translation: "The River," "Angleton" and "Rushdie" in my book *Invenciones de papel* (Ediciones Vuelta, 1990); six essays in *Vuelta* magazine; two in *Mandorla;* and "Paz in Asia" in the catalog to the exhibition "Octavio Paz: Los privilegios de la vista" at the Centro Cultural/Arte Contemporaneo in Mexico City. "Huidobro's *Altazor*" is expanded from the introduction to *Altazor* by Vicente Huidobro (Graywolf Press, 1988). "The Camera People" was written for the "Beyond Document" series at the Harvard Film Archive. "Everything dead trembles" accompanied an exhibition by Cecilia Vicuña at the Exit Art Gallery in New York City in 1990. "Dreams from the Holothurians" first appeared in Catalan translation in the catalog to an exhibition by Brian Nissen, "Atlantida," in Barcelona in 1992. Six of the essays first appeared in *Sulfur*. Others were first published in *The Boston Review, Conjunctions, The Hungry Mind Review, Index on Censorship, The Literary Review, Oblek* and *Transition*. All of the essays have been rewritten since these first appearances.

Manufactured in the United States of America
New Directions Books are printed on acid-free paper.
First published as New Directions Paperbook in 1992
Published simultaneously in Canada by Penguin Books Canada Limited

Library of Congress Cataloging in Publication Data

Weinberger, Eliot.
    Outside stories, 1987–1991 / Eliot Weinberger.
      p.   cm.
    ISBN 0–8112–1221–1 (pbk.)
    I. Title.
PS3573.E3928098   1992
814'.54—dc20

                                                              92–9869
                                                              CIP

New Directions Books are published for James Laughlin
by New Directions Publishing Corporation,
80 Eighth Avenue, New York 10011

CONTENTS

"Every line is the axis of a world."
—Novalis

for N.S., A.D. & S.

One

RIVERS OF POETRIES

THE RIVER

Having destroyed the Indus valley cities of Harappa and Mohenjo-daro, the tribes of warrior-shepherds we call the Aryans moved eastward into the Punjab and the foothills of the Himalayas. There, around 1500 B.C., in small villages—they hated cities—on the fertile banks of the Sarasvati River, the Aryan priests composed the sacred hymns, historical chronicles, mythological narratives, and prescriptions for ritual now known as the Vedas.

In the early Vedas, the Sarasvati, not surprisingly, was the literal and figurative life-source of the people: mother, goddess, vehicle for trade, origin of gold, metaphor for blood, sap, milk, and semen. Within 500 years, however, that fountain of life had dried up, completely disappeared, and the Aryans migrated further east, to two other great rivers, the Yamuna and the Ganga (Ganges).

By 900 B.C.—the time of the later Vedas and the mythological treatises, the *Brahmanas*—the vanished river had become both the lost river of memory and nostalgia, and a quite real, but now invisible, body of water. The confluence of the three rivers—Ganga, Yamuna, and Sarasvati, representing heaven, earth, and the underworld—is still celebrated in Allahabad, where it is believed that the third river becomes visible to the enlightened.

Simultaneous to her geographical and mythological disappearance, Sarasvati, the river and the river goddess, had yet another transformation. She became, and remains today, the mother of poetry.

The modern has been the great age of an invented and generalized archaic, our poetry and all the arts filled with evocations and the bric-a-brac of ancient civilizations and the contemporary indigenous peoples we consider as still living the ancient ways.

The archaic has been our escape from the monstrosities of the century; in the words (and antique spelling) of Ezra Pound: "Only antient wisdom is/solace to man's miseries." And more than solace: there has been a secret belief that if we could only untangle the mysteries of what happened at the beginning—the origins of the universe, of mankind, of speech, of society, of cities—that if we could recover the beginning of the story we could start it over again, correcting the evident mistakes that have brought us here.

Guy Davenport has written that "what was most modern in our times was what was most archaic." But more: what was most archaic was the longing for the archaic. For poetry—to speak only of poetry—regardless when, rises and has always risen from that vanished, sometimes banished river. At the most archaic (surviving) moment of every literature is a celebration of, or a nostalgia for, their own archaic.

In the beginning is the invention of the beginning. Every society has its epic, its "tale of the tribe," its invention of "us." In many ways, there is no "us" until "us" has created its own poetry. And it always begins at the beginning: the origin of the universe, followed in turn by an age of gods (now lost and usually lamented), the creation of man, and the founding of one's own people, who are celebrated for their rites and accomplishments (ancient valorization for current practices), their legendary or historical heroes. There are descents to the kingdom of the dead to learn the wisdom of "our" departed. And, most important, there is the definition of "us" by contrast to the (usually subjugated) "others." That description of the "others" is, however propagandistic, the first ethnography, the admission of the alien into the discourse, the beginning of the continuing nourishing of a culture.

When a literature shifts from oral to written, from collective to individual and undated to dated authorship, this function shifts from a definition of a timeless "us" to a definition of "us in the present"—the way we live now—as imagined by its writer. And, in the parallelism that is the dominant form of nearly all early poetry, the present is always, as might be expected, yoked to the past. It is a present that is either wanting (we have lost the river) or, at best, unstable (we may have our river, but someday it too will be lost)—an instability that is implicit even in moments of glory.

Sarasvati, pure water. Sarasvati dressed in white, her face rubbed white with sandalwood paste. The brightness of a thousand moons. Sarasvati astride her swan. Sarasvati who never marries. Sarasvati seated on a white lotus, floating above the mud of the world. Sarasvati, a blank page.

Small wonder that Pound's lines are themselves "antient wisdom." They come from his translation of the earliest surviving ethnopoetics anthology, the *Shih Ching,* the *Book of Odes* or *Songs,* and their guiding spirit Confucius is not only the most ancient (of whom we have records), but also the quintessential inventor of the archaic.

The 305 anonymous songs of the *Shih Ching* are a selection, reputedly made by Confucius himself, from a collection of over 3,000. At the time the anthology was edited, around 500 B.C., these songs were already at least 300 to 700 years old. (They had originally been collected for the Chou emperors as a way for the central government to find out what the people were thinking.) As they were gathered from all over China, many of them had to be translated from their local dialects, or otherwise adjusted so that their melodies would fit the standard Chinese of the time.

The purpose of the *Shih Ching* is, in certain ways, similar to Johann Gottfried von Herder's *Volkslieder* (1778) or Jerome Rothenberg's *Technicians of the Sacred* (1967)—to take two other famous anthologies of the "primitive." All three attempted a recovery of the wisdom of the "folk," the archaic "us," and both Rothenberg and Confucius—across their millennia—were presenting models *for use* of how poetry could be written. Furthermore, all three were self-consciously oppositional: Herder and Rothenberg to the prevailing classical canons (one in the service of German nationalism, the other to present an alternate lineage

for modernism), Confucius and Herder to the decadence of the
present. All three books were not anthologies in the original
sense of the word—a gathering of the prettiest flowers in the
field—but rather attempts to grasp and hold on to a small piece
of that which was receding.

Once there were sounds that created the world, that could
change the world. For some, the sounds were the names of gods.
In the beginning was the Word, the Maya gods standing in the
water, in darkness, Beckett characters talking the world into being. The Kabbalists claimed that the entire Torah was the name
of God—who could say it all at once? The Vedas, similarly, are a
transcription, a translation, a dilution of a single syllable that was
elaborated by Viyasa, their mythical creator.

Prayer, chant, mantra, formula, poem: concentrated, rhyth-
mical speech: Olson's "contruct of energy." All attempt to recover that original force of sound. Metaphor: a circumvention of
taboo sounds, the only way to name the unnamable. God: the
metaphor for God.

Confucius' anthology remained the central book of Chinese
poetry for 2,500 years, until the birth of the Republic in the
beginning of this century. (It survived the book-burnings of the
3rd century B.C. because it had been memorized by so many.)
Not only as an image-bank and a catalog of prosodic models, its
intrinsic relation to the past itself dominated the poetry for those
millennia.

For Confucius, a human ancestor is a divinity, and the past
represents the achievement of a terrestrial order (reflective of
the cosmic order) which has never again been accomplished, but
could be. The past is a present absence, an object of desire. Moreover, it is an object of desire that is manifest in objects, remnants,
relics. Chinese poetry, both early and late, is full of meditations
on ruins. There are hundreds of poems about finding some
artifact from the past, and thousands about remembering,
and remembering those who, in history, are famous for remembering.

The Chinese poet, in his or her most typical persona, is alone somewhere in the Empire: in exile, on a government mission to the provinces, in religious seclusion, or—for a woman—at home with her lover or husband away. It is a metaphor for the individual in the vastness of history. A product of separation, the Chinese poem was conceived as a fragment, a work that is permanently—like the final hexagram of the *I Ching*—"before completion." There are no Chinese epics—the closest it gets is the *T'ien wen,* a book of questions without answers—and the Chinese lyric always deliberately says less than it could. Even within the individual lines of the lyric fragment there are so-called "empty" (meaningless) words, through which the *ch'i* (the breath or the spirit) is meant to circulate through the poem, like wind in a ruins. And classical literary Chinese itself is so condensed that there are (particularly for Westerners) enormous gaps between the words—gaps that must be mentally filled, like broken pieces of cuneiform.

The English Romantics, following Volney, saw ruins as an allegorical emblem for the rise and fall of empires, the transience of human works, and the permanence of nature. They, like the Chinese, saw ruins as a triumph of chaos over order, which, unlike the Chinese, they further extrapolated into a mind-heart dichotomy. The Imagists—with their preference, unlike the Renaissance, for an unrestored Hellenism—proclaimed the ruin and the fragment as proof of the endurance of art. The headless, armless Venus was still beautiful; a poem of only four surviving words ("Spring . . ./ Too long . . ./ Gongula . . .") could still say it all. The Chinese imagined the fragment as a relic by which one mentally constructs the lost whole—the reader, as is now said, participating in the creation of the text. Like the moderns, they felt that the fragment was all that could be accomplished. Though their individual poems are not, like the moderns, assemblages of fragments, their language itself was.

Sarasvati, like all Hindu gods, has many names: Goddess of Speech, Living at the Front of the Tongue, She Who Lives on the Tongues of Poets, She Who Lives in Sound, The Power of Memory, The Power of Knowledge, She Whose Power Is the Power of Intellect, She Who Is the Power of Forming Ideas, She Who Is Intelligence.

Memory, knowledge, intellect: There is a beautiful, if not believable, theory of the origin of language advanced by certain paleolinguists. That language did not arise from the need to communicate—"I'm hungry" or Eat!" or "Look out!" or, the question that can't be answered, "Who's there?"—but rather from the need to think. Just as the visual system, from retina to cortex, produces a pictorial representation of the world, so language evolved to represent that which could not be seen—beginning, for protection's sake, with cause and effect. The origin of language, then, becomes identical to the act of writing: it is how one discovers what one knows, and is only secondarily its record.

Since the middle of the 18th century what has changed in poetry is only that the manifestations, the emanations, of the archaic and the "other" have multiplied along with the increasing archeological and ethnographic information. For the last 250 years we have meditated more on exotic than local ruins. The earliest past with which we speak—and, like the telescopic memories of old people, it is always the earliest moment that seems most vivid—continues to be pushed back, now to the Paleolithic. Our "others" are no longer the subjugated neighbors, but a wide range of (equally subjugated) peoples—though the modern poet, unlike the poets from the archaic to the end of the European colonial empires, takes no pride in that subjugation, believing that the "other" is only another form of "us." Like everything else, it is a supermarket of choices: ancient and foreign images, mythologies, rites, practices, philosophies, from which the individual discovers the ideas and objects of an idiosyncratic rapport: emblems of the universal human, an "us" to which one goes on pilgrimage to find the "I."

I thought, suddenly, of the mass animal sacrifices I had attended a few years before in a valley outside of Kathmandu.

Hundreds of the faithful snaked in a single file over the hills: the men leading male kids on a tether; the women with roosters and plates heaped with yellow and red flowers, incense, and clarified butter; the poorest among them holding a single egg dipped in blood. At the bottom of the ravine was an altar open on four sides, canopied by the hoods of four enormous gilt cobras. There a spring came out of the ground, and there too was the object of veneration: Kali, goddess of death and destruction, grinning, squatting on a prostrate corpse, with her legs spread and a skull cup between her thighs. One by one the priests decapitated the animals, splattered the blood on the image of the goddess, and carried the carcasses to the blood-red stream to be washed and cooked in huge simmering pots, the meat fed to the pilgrims.

As described thus far, it was a scene that the modern, urban connoisseur of the archaic has learned how to read. Birth and death and rebirth, cosmic time: Mother Earth (with her spring and open altar) turning into Mother Death (giving birth to a skull, demanding the blood of males) and back to Mother Earth again (the meat of the sacrifice nourishing the faithful). If Sarasvati is the continuing life of the mind, Kali is the eternal decay, death, and rebirth of the body.

But what struck me most about the rite was its utter ordinariness. Here were not only peasants in traditional dress, but also men in polyester suits. Teenagers carried boom-boxes, families were having boisterous picnics, small groups of men played cards. The mood was, above all, that of a Sunday outing.

The modern invention of the archaic has projected an aura of drama and solemnity onto traditional religious practice—a kind of mental Gothic cathedral for the forest where the rites are enacted and the myths told. And when the boom-boxes start appearing at the animal sacrifice, it is seen as a dilution of the past, a weakening of the faith.

Yet an essential quality of the archaic is precisely its lack of distinction between sacred and profane—its habitual daily commerce between the gods and the people. It is a sign of religious decadence when that exchange is relegated to a single hour of the week in a separate (and silent) house. To recover the ancient power of poetry, one must begin by recognizing that the ancient formulae, the sacred chants, were sounds that occurred—that still occur—amidst a general noise. To complain about the racket drowning out poetry is to imagine a past that never existed. Poetry is not a secret rite: it is a public act that is generally ignored. But if it were to disappear—and who knows, it has never happened—the worlds it organizes into speech might well vanish with it.

The invention of an archaic, the opening of the poem to the "other," is not merely the essential modernist enterprise: it is a primary activity of poetry itself. Metaphor: "to move from one place to another." The poem is not a vehicle, it is an act of transportation (if we can scrape away the fossil-fuel encrustations on that word). The poem, made of breath, blows us away— to everything that is not "us," to everything by which an "us" is created. Writer to reader, self to another self, living to the dead, city to another city, metropolis to nature, today to yesterday, this world to other worlds. Silence to sound to silence: the Hindu history of the universe. Louis Zukofsky—following Dante's belief that things move to recover what they lack, to correct a defect— writes: "Properly no verse should be called a poem if it does not convey the totality of perfect rest." But he's wrong: the condition a poem aspires to is not absolute stillness, the ataraxia of ascetics, but rather a state of perpetual motion. Art, said Louis Sullivan, does not fulfill desire, it creates desire. Stillness is death: the river turned to a pool. Robert Duncan, in his last poem:

In the real I have always known myself
　　　in this realm where no Wind　　　stirs
　　　　　no Night
turns in turn to Day,　　　the Pool of the motionless water,
　　　the absolute Stillness.　　In the World, death after
　　　　　　　　　　　　　　　　　　　　　death.

In this realm,　　　no last thrall of Life stirs.
　　　The imagination alone knows this condition.
　　　As if this were before the War,　　before

What Is,   in the dark this state
that knows nor sleep nor waking, nor dream
        —an eternal arrest.

Our time is no longer a cycle or a linear progression, but, like
our myth of the creation of the universe, an omnidirectional "big
bang." Bits of the past fly all around us: we ricochet off them as
we hurtle with them into the nothing. (The projectivist poem,
with its "field" composition, is a map of time.) And yet the poem
remains, as it always has been, a hymn to, and a dream of, its
vanished or invisible river, its lost or unexploded time. A poetry
without its own archaic, that doesn't talk with the dead, that
doesn't meditate on ruins, that doesn't know it is surrounded by
others who contradict everything it says, that has no nostalgia—a
poem, in other words, that is still, completed, in eternal arrest—
can only exist at the end of Christian or Hindu or Confucian or
Aztec time, when poetry will no longer be written. Beauty, said
Breton—his "convulsive beauty"—arises from the tension between stillness and motion: a locomotive engine abandoned to
the jungle, tangled with growth.

The only ending is a longing for ending. Edmund Spenser, a
Christian and a self-conscious archaicist, abandons his epic with a
truncated "unperfite" canto that yearns for completion:

For all that moveth doth in change delight:
But thence-forth all shall rest eternally
With Him that is the God of Sabbaoth hight:
O that great Sabbaoth God graunt me that Sabaoths sight!

Even Dante, who was granted that sight, could only end his
geometrically perfect poem lamenting the inadequacies of
speech. For the vision of God erases memory—Dante compares
it to a dream: its details lost, only some small sense of great
passion remaining—and language without memory, an amnesiac
poetry, cannot exist. His Paradise must remain a blank space, a
silence, outlined by the poem: its final metaphor is a geometer
who cannot understand the circle he has drawn.

Spenser's best poem, "Prothalamion," celebrates an as-yet-unperformed marriage, like the couples in Bosch's garden, for-ever frozen in the moment before copulation, a poem that turns on an ironic refrain: "Sweete Themmes, runne softly, till I end my song." Ironic for, if the river ended when his song ended, if river and song ever ended, if we ever reached the future, we would reach the end.

[1988]

HUIDOBRO'S *ALTAZOR*

Yes, the imagination, drunk with prohibitions, has destroyed and recreated everything afresh in the likeness of that which it was. Now indeed men look about in amazement at each other with a full realization of the meaning of "art."

—William Carlos Williams, 1923

Alto, high; *azor,* hawk. *Altazor,* a poem in seven cantos, written by a Chilean living in Paris. Begun in 1919 and published in 1931, the poem spans most of those extraordinarily optimistic years between two global disasters. An age that thought itself post-apocalyptic: the war to end all wars was fought and over, and now there was a new world to create. A time when the West was, literally and figuratively, electrified; when the mass production of telephones, automobiles, movies, record players, toasters, radios, skyscrapers, airplanes, bridges, cameras, blimps, and subways matched an aesthetic production obsessed with celebrating the new, an aesthetics that (in Margaret Bourke-White's famous remark) found dynamos more beautiful than pearls. Painters, sculptors, and photographers saw their task as making the new out of the new, dismantling and reassembling everything from eggbeaters to spark plugs to the Hoover Dam. Poets, the citizens of international progress, wrote in other languages or invented their own. Cinematic jumpcuts, verbal and visual Cubism, simultaneity and collage: on the page and on the canvas, all time collapsed into the single moment of now. "Speed," said Norman Bel Geddes, who redesigned the world, "is the cry of our era," and *Altazor* is, among other things, surely the fastest-reading long poem ever written. What other poem keeps reminding us to hurry up, that there's no time to lose?

Vicente Huidobro (1893–1948) arrived in Paris in 1916 and

stayed in the thick of it. Trilingual poet, novelist, screenplay writer, war correspondent, painter, propagandist, self-promoter, founder of newspapers and literary magazines (the first, *Nord-Sud,* edited with Apollinaire and Reverdy), candidate for President of Chile. He is the least-known member of the Spanish-American quaternity, with Vallejo, Neruda, and Paz. (Pound wanted to translate him in the early 1920s; it took another fifty years for a book to appear in English.) His biography, alas, has never been adequately written, but his portrait was painted by Picasso, Gris, and Arp.

"Contemporary poetry," he wrote, "begins with me," and, at least for his own language, it was no exaggeration: his Cubist poems of 1917 and 1918, exploding over the page, effectively pulled Spanish poetry out of its symbolist *modernismo* and into international modernism. Huidobro's banner, in the proliferation of isms, was Creationism—a movement of which he was the only member—which declared that poetry, the gloss on or simulacrum of reality, was dead. In the new world, the poets, "little gods," would invent their own worlds: "Why sing of roses, oh Poets? Make them bloom in the poem." It was a movement that was simultaneously modern, in its belief that in the new era human imagination would be able to do anything, and archaic, reflecting the contemporary preoccupation with the "primitive," particularly the spells and charms of sympathetic magic. Whether or not he succeeded in making the roses bloom—and who's to say?—Huidobro did make them speak, and in their own language.

His masterpiece was *Altazor,* a poem that begins in the ruins of the war—the date 1919 appears on the title page to locate the poem, not its composition—and rushes headlong into the future, as its hero, Altazor, the "antipoet," hurtles through space. The century's great paean to flight, its unnamed icon is Charles Lindbergh (to whom Huidobro attempted to erect a monument in New York—with $10,000 in prize money from the Hollywood League for Better Pictures—and about whom he wrote a still-unpublished long poem in English). In *Altazor* the high-hawk aeronaut is the new Christ, the liberator, and the airplane his

Cross: not as an agent of suffering, but as a vehicle for ascension. It is curious that the American expatriate poet and sun-worshipper Harry Crosby described watching Lindbergh's landing in his diaries (unpublished until 1977) in precisely these terms:

> Then sharp swift in the gold glare of the searchlights a small white hawk of a plane swoops hawk-like down and across the field—C'est lui Lindbergh, LINDBERGH! and there is pandemonium wild animals let loose and a stampede toward the plane . . . and it seems as if all the hands in the world are touching or trying to touch the new Christ and that the new Cross is the Plane . . . Ce n'est pas un homme, c'est un Oiseau!

Most of all, the new Christ was taking us not to the moon and stars of the ballads, but into Einstein space, a place where speed is capable of telescoping time, but where the obstacle to total simultaneity is mass. (The weight of the writing will forever keep the simultaneous poem from being written.) *Altazor* is a poem of falling, not back to earth—though certain critics have insisted on reading it as a version of the Icarus myth—but out into space. The faster Altazor falls, the faster the poem reads. As his body burns up like a meteor, mass transforming into energy, all ages become contemporaneous, the tombs open—the poem is also a product of Tutmania—and all places become one. Above all, the old language of poetry is consumed with the body of the poet, and a new language, progressively more radical is created out of puns, neologisms, pages of identical rhymes (his 250 variations on "windmill" an homage to Rabelais' "balls"), animal and plant dialects. By the last canto, the poet has become pure energy, a language of pure sound: contrary to the Pentecost, the poet has risen into, has become, the tongues of flame. Altazor is both an archaic shaman, leaving his body to travel to other worlds, and the new aeronaut who, like the polar explorers—and Huidobro was crazy about polar explorers—travels into the realms of nothingness, the "infiniternity," regardless of the small hope of coming back:

Ahee ah ee aheee ah ee ee ee ee oh eeah

Alto, high, *azor,* hawk. Or is it an anagram for *Alsator,* Shelley's long poem of "a youth of uncorrupted feelings and adventurous genius led forth by an imagination inflamed and purified through familiarity with all that is excellent and majestic, to the contemplation of the universe"? Shelley's Romantic poet-hero, first at peace with the "infinite and unmeasured," grows dissatisfied with eternity, and in the end is literally consumed, killed, by desire for the Other he has invented in his total solitude. Huidobro's Nietzschean anti-poet/hero, abandons his Other (the incongruous love of Canto II) to reach satori in the pure energy of pure language.

[Pure language: even before the language (languages) the poet invents, there is the mystery of what known language the poem was written in. Fragments were first published in French; the book finally in Spanish. The nightingale of the poem—whose middle syllable runs through the musical scale—is not a Spanish *ruiseñor* but a French *rossignol* made Spanish: *rosiñol.* Thus a poem that nearly all critics have pronounced untranslatable may itself be a translation.]

"All the languages are dead," he wrote, and so was "poetical poetry poetry." In the future poems would be written in bird-language, star-language, airplane-language, and we would all inhabit a "beautiful madness in the zone of language." For decades it was thought that *Altazor* was a noble disaster that admitted its own failure by its descent into gibberish. Lately the postmoderns have used it as a prophesy of their revelation of the fundamental meaninglessness of language. This wasn't what he meant at all: once upon a time, the new was sacred, and the future the only mythical era.

[1988]

PAZ IN ASIA

1. A Continent of Poets

Paul Claudel went to China with the Foreign Service, and the century begins with his *Connaissance de l'Est* [Knowledge of the East, 1900]: "I understand the harmony of the world; when will I grasp its melody?"

Victor Segalen went to China as a medical officer and wrote a history of the stone statues. He printed his *Stèles* (1912), Chinese fashion, on the press of the Lazarite Fathers in Beidang: poems, semi-disguised as translations, that sought to "transfer the Chinese Empire to the Empire of the Self"; poems that would be as timeless, impassive, monumental, ceremonial as the slowly eroding characters carved on the funerary tablets; poems that "do not express: that signify, that are."

Arthur Waley never went to Asia, never learned to speak a word of Chinese or Japanese, and spent his life listening to that silence and recreating what he heard.

Ezra Pound never went to Asia: he constructed his own continent of texts, inventing the languages from which, and to which, they were translated. As a student he found the word "vortex" in the pamphlets on Hinduism he gave his fiancée, Hilda Doolittle; he practiced yogic breathing all his life; he believed in an idiosyncratic version of *kundalini* he had picked up in Remy de Gourmont. From the manuscripts he inherited from the Orientalist Ernest Fenollosa, he translated Nō plays, having little idea of their form, but finding in them the model for "a long poem in free verse, a long Imagiste poem." A model that would become the *Cantos* and, among so many things, encompass the dynastic history of China, as written by the French. He believed, with Fenollosa, that Chi-nese was the "ideal language of the world," a language whose writing was a direct representation of the thing expressed; that the "ideogram," like a poem, brought language back to its archaic concreteness. Translating the Chinese poems translated for Fenollosa by a Japanese informant, he repeated many of their mistakes; others he intuitively corrected. He found his ideal social order in Confucius, found a Confucian rectitude in Jefferson and Mussolini, hated "Taozers" and "Budhs." In the madhouse he wrote a strange and magnificent ideogrammic translation of the *Book of Odes*, incorporating his own pseudo-etymologies in the text. In his last years, unable to marry a young disciple, he was absorbed in the love-suicide poems and the religious rituals of the Na-khi people on the Tibetan border: "without ²Mùan ¹bpö/ no reality."

W. B. Yeats never went to Asia, but he shared a cottage with Pound as the Fenollosa papers were being rewritten, and invented his own form of Irish Nō, based on Celtic myth and the dances he'd seen of Michio Ito, though Ito was attempting to jettison Japanese tradition. He believed in the Aryan myth, a net of cultural correspondences stretching from Dublin to Benares, and placed the Hindu swastika on the title pages of his books. In his last years he planned to go to India with Sri Purohit Swami, but his health was poor. They went to Mallorca instead, and translated ten of the *Upanishads*.

Hu Shih went to Chicago in 1913, read the issue of *Poetry* with Pound's "A Few Don'ts by an Imagiste" and returned to China to publish a nearly identical "Tentative Proposals for the Improvement of Literature"—finding in the West what Pound thought he had found in the East—a manifesto that set off the literary revolution of the May Fourth Movement of 1919.

Blaise Cendrars claimed he went to China, where the Chinese had changed his pseudonym from Braise Cendrart (ember-ash-art). His masterpiece, "Prose of the Transsiberian" (1913), recounts a trip across Russia and Mongolia to Harbin, Manchuria; it is doubtful he ever went. His 1914 poem "Bombay Express" is equally imaginary, and memorable for two immortal lines: "This year or next/art criticism is as stupid as esperanto."

Rainer Maria Rilke never went to Asia, but he took a carving of the Buddha—as he took nearly everything—as a metaphor for the artist, enclosing the universe within, long after the stars are dead.

Raymond Roussel went to China and India in 1920, but rarely opened the shutters of his steamer cabins or his hotel rooms.

Max Jacob never went to Asia, but he declared, oh scandal, that three lines of any haiku were infinitely superior to the three hundred pages of Péguy's *Eve*.

T. S. Eliot never went to Asia, but he studied Sanskrit and Pali at Harvard, considered converting to Buddhism, and embedded bits of the *Upanishads* and the sermons of the Buddha in *The Waste Land*, and the *Bhagavad-Gita* in the *Four Quartets*. "And I came to the conclusion . . . that my only hope of really penetrating to the heart of that mystery would lie in forgetting how to think and feel as an American or a European: which, for practical as well as sentimental reasons, I did not wish to do."

Takamura Kōtarō saw a photograph of Rodin's "Poetry" and knew he had to get out. In 1906 he left Tokyo for New York, London, and Paris, discovered Baudelaire, Rimbaud, and the Symbolists, and returned three years later, bringing the vernacular and *vers libre* to Japanese poetry.

Saint-John Perse went to China in the 1920s as a diplomat, predicted a peasant revolution, and wrote, in prose poetry, the history of the conquest of an imaginary Central Asian kingdom, *Anabasis* (1924), which both Eliot and Walter Benjamin translated, and which, in the late twenties and thirties, launched a thousand young poets.

Pablo Neruda spent five years in the foreign service in Burma, Ceylon, India, and Singapore, miserable, speaking little English, and writing the poems of his best book, *Residence on Earth* (1931 and 1935): poems that are notable for containing nearly nothing Asian in them.

Louis Zukofsky never went to Asia, but he found his initials—and what other poet so loved his own initials?—in the calligraphic signature of the Zen monk Ryōkan. The fourth section of his life-work *"A"* includes his translation of a "Japanese" poem by the Yiddish poet Samuel Bloomgarden ("Yehoash"): "Shimaunu-San, Samurai, / When will you come home?"

Bertolt Brecht and Antonin Artaud never went to Asia, and never met, but at the same moment they discovered Eastern theater: a performance of Kabuki in Berlin, a Balinese troupe in Paris. For both it was the revelation of a ritualistic theater that was purely physical, that transcended language and eliminated stage artifice; from it they derived their dissimilar theories of alienation effect and cruelty. Brecht rewrote Arthur Waley's rewriting of Zenchiku's Nō play *Taniko* as *He Who Says Yes* (1929), and then rewrote it again as *He Who Says No* (1930). He took a bad translation of Li Hsing Tao's 13th-century play *The Chalk Circle* and set it in the Caucasus; his *Man Is Man* (1925) comes from Kipling's Raj; three of his other plays—notably *The Good Woman of Setzuan* (1940)—are set in China. Late in his life he translated some of Waley's translations of Po Chü-i, and among the papers left after his death was a scene from an unfinished play, *The Life of Confucius,* to be performed entirely by children.

Artaud never met the Dalai Lama, but he wrote him letters: "We are your faithful servants, O Grand Lama, give us, grace us with your illuminations in a language our contaminated minds can understand . . ."

[Allen Ginsberg and Gary Snyder met the Dalai Lama, though a different incarnation, who asked them about hallucinogenic mushrooms.]

W. H. Auden went to China with Christopher Isherwood during the Japanese War, wrote some of his worst poems, and read Trollope in a bunker as the bombs exploded around him.

William Empson lived in China for years, and wrote four pages of prose to explain the 28 lines of his poem called "China," in which, for example, the phrase "Cheese crumbles" meant that in the 1930s "the prolonged disorder of China made everything feel crumbling like cheese."

Dai Wangshu went to France in 1932, met Breton and Jacob, interviewed Supervielle, borrowed money from Malraux, sat at the feet of Gide and Éluard, went to Spain to find Alberti, Salinas, and Lorca. His magazine in China, *Xiandai: Les Contemporaines,* began publishing a few months after the Mexican magazine *Contemporaneos* closed: both published many of the same French and Spanish poets. Dai's translations would have their greatest effect fifty years later, among the young poets looking for a way out of social realism.

Basil Bunting never went east of Persia, but he rewrote Kamo no Chōmei's prose memoir of the disasters in Kyoto in the 1180s, and for years the only Bunting scholars were in Japan.

Henri Michaux went everywhere in Asia, a parody of the outsider, a self-styled "barbarian" devoted to the sweetness of the particular and countless sour generalizations. The century's most radical translator of Chinese poetry, he took the written page, "which, covered with characters turns into something crammed and seething, full of lives and objects, of everything to be found in the world . . . clustered that they might end in ideas or unravel in poetry" and freed the signs of their signification, inventing a calligraphy for a language (languages) "far from words, far from other people's words."

William Carlos Williams never went to Asia, but before his death he translated nearly forty Chinese poems, working with David Rafael Wang, at the time the only Chinese White Supremacist in America, and later the only Chinese Black Panther.

Vicente Huidobro never went to Asia, but sitting in Paris in the 1920s he wondered: "When I move my left foot / What is the great Chinese mandarin doing with his foot?"

Hugh MacDiarmid went to China in 1956, met Mao, and gave a public reading under enormous portraits of Blake and Whitman. He wrote the history of Western translations of Sanskrit as a six-page poem.

Charles Olson never went to Asia, but he mysteriously inserted the words of Mao, in French—as Pound had received his Chinese history from the French—into "The Kingfishers," and placed various Hindu gods in the niches of his *Maximus.* Falling asleep reading *The Secret of the Golden Flower,* the 9th-century Chinese alchemical text favored by Jungians, he received "a gift of the truth": a low voice repeating over and over a single sentence: "Everything issues from the Black Chrysanthemum, and nothing is anything but itself measured so."

The Spanish poets never went to Asia, for they found their Orient nearer, across the Strait of Gibraltar, and in their blood. But Juan Ramón Jiménez, Antonio Machado, and Federico García Lorca, in the haiku craze of the teens and twenties, wrote short lyrics that were a conjunction of Japanese poetry and local folk songs, and Jiménez translated Tagore, a book that would be imitated—some would say plagiarized—by the young Neruda.

Kenneth Rexroth went to Japan often, reimagined Chinese and Japanese poetry as it might have been written in the California Sierras, and in the last years of his life wrote the erotic poems of a young Japanese woman, Marichiko, whom he had invented.

Charles Reznikoff never went anywhere, but thought his poetics were most perfectly articulated by the Sung Dynasty poet Wei T'ai: "Poetry presents the thing in order to convey the feeling. It should be precise about the thing and reticent about the feeling."

André Breton never went to Asia, but he read haiku and Suzuki, compared automatic writing to meditation, found Zen inferior to Surrealism, and thought the word Orient corresponded to the "anguish of these times, to its secret hope."

George Oppen never went to Asia, but in his only translation he collaborated on versions from the Bengali of poems in praise of the Goddess: "Words, there are words! / But with your eyes / We see . . ."

And the Chinese translations of the British

Museum's Assistant Keeper of Oriental Antiquities, Soame Jenyns, descendant of Soame Jenyns, the 18th-century optimist ridiculed by Johnson, were rewritten by the young Paul Blackburn, hitchhiking to St. Elizabeths to visit Pound.

René Daumal went to India in the 1920s, became the secretary to the Uday Shankar classical dance troupe, learned Sanskrit, and was the only poet of the century to directly translate the sacred texts and write on Indian poetics: "Crippled in the chaos of the Occident, without a connecting thread, I can only wish to play the necrologist-poet to an inimical culture. The Orient is still alive . . . But the Occidental free-arbitrary-dualist-individualist, the sad capitalist-colonialist-imperialist, fettered with the etiquette of his order—he is finished."

As Robert Duncan's mother put the boy to bed reading Bashō.

For poets, the project of the 20th century has been the discovery of all that poetry is not (but could be) and the recovery of all that poetry (it is imagined) was. Pound predicted that the century's poets would find its "new Greece" in the East: there lay the greatest wealth of untranslated literature, and an ancient world that was almost new. To write the poem that had never been, a place to begin was the people who were not us.

2. Transpacific Express

> Nous ne pouvons pas aller au Japon
> Viens au Mexique!
> Blaise (Braise) Cendrars

Did these ancestors really meet, or did they merely sing to each other, like whales, across the Pacific Basin? There were no Maya

Boddhisattvas; no one in Anyang had his heart cut out to feed the sun. And yet what they made looks and does not look the same:

felines holding tiny figures in their paws; the chinless feathered monster headdresses; bracelets of open jaws; the diamond-patterned skirts; the loincloth aprons hanging from a monster mask; the anthropomorphic beings emerging from the mouths of long-snouted double-headed creatures; the serpent arches, framing a seated figure, with a mask at the apex; cross-legged deities; gods with three faces; the double-headed serpent held across the chest, and the serpent's Ho Chi Minh beard; gods with vertical stacked heads; the knee-length beads; the umbrella staffs; the high looping hairdos; the figures standing on the backs of slaves or demons; the two profile heads that form a frontal face; the masks on the façades of the buildings; the maize god in the Boon-Bestowing *mudra;* the seated figures flanked by fat dwarfs and topped with winged creatures; and—

could that really be an elephant carved on a stela in Copan?

Felipe de las Casas, son of a wealthy merchant, sails from Acapulco to Manila in 1590 to seek his fortune and taste the legendary vices. He next appears, four years later, at the doors of a Franciscan monastery, begging to be admitted to the order. His piety is great. In 1596 he is sent back to Mexico to preach. His ship, the *San Felipe,* is lost and more lost in a series of storms. It washes up on the coast of Japan. The Shōgun, having reluctantly permitted Christian missionaries in Nagasaki, now believes they are the cause of a recent earthquake. Felipe and twenty-six other priests are crucified by samurai. At that moment, back in Mexico, the dried branches of a fig tree in the family's patio are suddenly covered with leaves. From the wreck of the *San Felipe:* San Felipe, the first Mexican saint.

By 1600 there is more trade across the Pacific than the Atlantic: Mexican silver and gold, copper, chocolate, and cochineal, for

Asian silk, camel hair, mineral and vegetable inks, precious stones, jade, rattan, marble, paper, aromatic oils, cork, teak, feathers, camphor, amber, jet, alabaster, palm leaves for roofing, shells, furniture, porcelain, mother of pearl, and those pearls formed in the bellies of porcupines: the magical medicinal bezoar stones.

In the 17th century some 600 Asian immigrants arrive each year in Mexico. One of them is a 12-year-old Moghul princess of Delhi, who was kidnapped by pirates off the Malabar Coast. Sold in the Manila slave market, she is shipped to Acapulco and sold again to a pious couple from Puebla. Under the religious training of her owners, she soon becomes famous as an ascetic and mystic. She is known as Catarina de San Juan, *la china poblana* [the Chinese woman of Puebla]; many miracles are attributed to her.

An excellent seamstress, she embroiders her blouses and skirts with bright-colored flowers and birds. The fashion spreads throughout the country to become the "typical" Mexican dress. Its third component, the shawl, is imported from Gujarat in western India.

At the same moment, *mole,* the national dish, is invented by the nuns at the Puebla convent with which Catarina is associated. An array of chiles and spices are roasted and ground separately, and then combined with chocolate into a thick dark sauce. Though the ingredients are local, the process is unlike anything in Mexican cooking: it is, however, how Indian food is made.

In 1635 the Spanish barbers petition the Mexico City council to ask the Viceroy to drive the Oriental barbers out of the Plaza Mayor and other fashionable districts. The council refuses; they too want decent haircuts.

By 1703 there is a full-scale Asian market at the southwest corner of the Plaza Mayor, selling silks, brocade, fans, lace, marble boxes, watches, microscopes, porcelain, and painted screens. It will last until 1843.

In the 18th century, the currency of choice throughout China and Japan is the Mexican silver peso.

In 1888 Mexico and Japan open diplomatic relations. In 1896, the Mexican poet José Juan Tablada writes in a Japanese reverie: "Gilded mirage, opium dream, / fountain of all my ideals! / . . . / I am the slave of your Mikado! / I am the bonze of your pagodas!"[1] In 1897 the Society for the Japanese Colonization of Mexico sends its first settlers to Chiapas to build coffee plantations and a new town called Enomoto Takeaki.

As the century begins, Tablada has finally arrived in Tokyo, though the experience barely tempers his *japonaiserie*: "The night, the lake, and the moon / from her high balcony / the Princess Satsuna gazes / heady with opium and love."[2] He does, however, translate some tankas and utas which, though still full of Spanish modernist (our Symbolist) rhetoric, are among the earliest in the language. And he ends the second section of his poem "Musa Japonica"—inexplicably titled in Latin and dedicated to the "beloved one"—with a tercet composed entirely of dots, which is either avant-garde or coy.

He returns to Mexico with an enormous collection of *ukio-e* prints and antiques, and builds a Japanese wing to his house in Coyoacán, complete with rock garden. In 1914 he publishes a book on Hiroshige, the first in Spanish. Later that year the house is plundered by Zapatistas overthrowing the dictatorship of Victoriano Huerta, whom Tablada had supported; the poet goes into exile in New York ("You women who go by on Fifth Avenue, / so near to my eyes, so far from my life").[3] In 1918 his first book of poetry in nearly ten years includes only one poem connected to Japan, a heroic ballad

[1] ¡Aureo espejisimo, sueño de opio, / fuente de todos mis ideales! / . . . / ¡Yo soy el siervo de tu Mikado! / ¡Yo soy el bonzo de tus pagodas!

[2] La noche, el lago y la luna / desde el alto mirador / ve la princesa Satsuna / ebria de opio y de amor.

[3] Mujeres que pasáis por la Quinta Avenida, / tan cerca de mis ojos, tan lejos de mi vida.

on the printmaker Hokusai, most notable for its ingenious Spanish rhymes with Japanese words. The next year Tablada becomes Tablada with *One Day . . .* [Un dia . . .], subtitled
"Synthetic Poems," a small book of 38 haiku, written in Colombia
and dedicated to the poets Shiyo and Bashō. It is the first book of
original haiku written by a poet outside of Japan.

Though *One
Day . . .* is—with Huidobro's 1917 and 1918 publications, *The
Mirror of Water* [El espejo de agua], *Equatorial* [Ecuatorial], and
Arctic Poems [Poemas árcticos]—one of the earliest books of the
Spanish Vanguard (our modernism), the way to these haiku was
perhaps pointed by Pound's 1912 "In a Station of the Metro," or
Alfonso Reyes' 1913 "Euclides' haiku" ("Parallel lines / are con-
vergents / that meet only in infinity."),[1] or the short poems Juan
Ramón Jiménez was publishing in 1917 ("Book, the misfor-
tune / of being everywhere / alone!").[2] Whatever the case, Tablada—unlike the Mexican Efrén Rebolledo who, though he lived
for eight years in Japan and China, mainly incorporated exotic
images into the Symbolist fantasies of his *Japanese Rhymes* [Rimas
japoneses, 1907 and 1915]—succeeded in eliminating all of the
Oriental trappings, adapting the Japanese form to close observa-
tions of local flora and fauna. Tablada's remain among the most
memorable haiku in any language: *"Tierno saúz / casi oro, casi
ambar, / casi luz . . ."* [which, losing the rhyme on which the
poem turns, translates as: "Tender willow / almost golden, almost
amber / almost light . . ."]

In 1920 he publishes his book of
"ideographic" poems, *Li-Po and Other Poems* [Li-Po y otros
poemas]. The title poem continues Tablada's witty use of East-
West rhymes (*"mejor viajar / en palanquín / y hacer / un poema / sin
fín / en la torre / de Kaolín / de Nankín"*) ["better to travel / in a pala-
quin / and make / a poem / without end / in the tower / of Ka-
olin / in Nankin"], and a page of it is written in the shape of

---

[1] *Hai-kai de Euclides.* Líneas paralelas / son las convergentes / que sólo se juntan
en el infinito.

[2] ¡Libro, afán / de estar en todas partes, / en soledad!

the Chinese character for "longevity," a Taoist charm that had long since degenerated into a commercial good-luck emblem, like the Irish four-leafed clover. *Li-Po* is a book that contains, among others: the thinnest sonnet in Spanish[1]; a poem that must be held to a mirror to be read; a poem consisting almost entirely of nocturnal sounds; and the small simultaneist classic "Alternating nocturne":

> New York night gold
> > *Cold walls of Moorish lime*
> Rector's foxtrot champagne
> > *Mute houses and heavy gates*
> And looking back
> > *On the silent roofs*
> The soul petrified
> > *The white cats of the moon*
> Like Lot's wife

> > And nevertheless
> > > it is always
> > > > the same
> > > > > in New York
> > > > > > or Bogota

> > > MOON . . . ![2]

It is unlikely that Tablada had seen the four calligrammic "Summer Japonaiseries" [Japonerías de estío] Huidobro had privately published in Santiago de Chile in 1913, but surely he was aware, despite his later denials, of Apollinaire's *Calligrammes*.

---

[1] GO / ZA / BA / YO // A / BO / GO / TA // TE / MI / RE // Y / ME / FUI. [I enjoyed Bogota. I saw you and I left.] The rhyme scheme is ABBA, BAAB, CDC, DCD.

[2] *Nocturno Alterno*. Neoyorquina noche dorada / *Frios muros de cal moruna* / Rector's champaña fox-trot / *Casas mudas y fuertes rejas* / Y volviendo la mirada / *Sobre las silenciosas tejas* / El alma petrificada / *Los gatos blancos de la luna* / Como la mujer de Loth // Y sin embargo / es una / misma / en New York / y en Bogotá // LA LUNA . . . !

"Lettre-Océan" [Sea-Mail] appeared in *Les Soirées de Paris* in June 1914: given its Mexican subject matter, not to mention its Francophone variations on Mexican slang (*çingada,* indeed!), it was unlikely to have been missed by a Francophile like Tablada. The August issue of the magazine contained Apollinaire's "new-style" *calligrammes* in representational shapes (as most of Tablada's would be) and an article by the critic G. Arbouin on "Lettre-Océan" that was much discussed at the time. In his essay Arbouin declares that "it is necessary that our intelligence become accustomed to understanding synthetico-ideographically instead of analytico-discursively." Both of these key words, "synthetic" and "ideographic," would appear in the subtitles of *One Day . . .* and *Li-Po.* (Six months later, another Francophile, Ezra Pound, would use the word for the first time in an essay on "Imagisme and England": "We have sought the force of Chinese ideographs *without knowing it.*")

In 1922 Tablada publishes *The Jug of Flowers* [El jarro de flores], a book of 68 haiku, including his wittiest efforts ("The little monkey's looking at me . . . / He wants to tell me something / but forgot what it was!")[1] and an introduction where Tablada gives himself credit for introducing haiku into Spanish. He even hints that it is his influence which has led to the special 1920 issue of *Nouvelle Revue Française* on haiku—though that publication was merely the climax of some years of haiku-mania: a fad that received its official imprimatur with the appointment of Paul Claudel as Ambassador to Japan in 1921.

Regardless of Tablada's international effect, his importance to Mexico is unquestionable: José Gorostiza's 1925 *Songs to Sing in the Boats* [Canciones para cantar en las barcas] contains poems about Li Po and the Lady Yang Kuei-fei, and tiny lyrics such as "The Lighthouse," which reads in its entirety: "Light-haired shepherd of fishing boats."[2] The same year Jaime Torres Bodet publishes a book of haiku called *Folding Screen* [Biombo—

---

[1] El pequeño mono me mira . . . / ¡Quisiera decirme / algo que se le olvida!
[2] *El faro.* Rubio pastor de barcas pescadoras.

the Spanish word coming from the Japanese *byobu*, windbreak].
In 1926 Alfonso Reyes is writing "Afternoon": "Thin skin of the
clouds/where a sliver of moon/stuck, is walking"[1]; and Xavier
Villaurrutia's "Insomniac Suite" [Suite del insomnio] that same
year is a series of haiku.

And more haiku—it becomes a Mexican pastime—by Rafael
Lozano, Manuel Ponce, Carlos Pellicer, Efrain Huerta, Homero
Aridjis, Francisco Monterde, José Emilio Pacheco, and so many
others.
       Among them, the club Kuka-no-tsudoi, composed of Ja-
panese businessmen and diplomats, which has been meeting
monthly in Mexico City since 1955. After a dinner that combines
sashimi and *carnitas,* these amateurs declaim their own haiku,
such as: *Mariach/kanade chikazuku/yuuransen*
                                        that is: "Maria-
chis/play, coming nearer:/a pleasure-boat."

In Chinese and Japanese, the characters for "Mexico" mean:

COUNTRY OF INK

3. The figure in the landscape

As an adolescent, Octavio Paz discovers French modernism in
Anabasis. A 1945 memorial essay on Tablada, emphasizing both
the haiku and Mexican motifs, hopes to rescue the poet from
oblivion—though the poems will remain out of print for nearly
thirty more years. In 1952, his first visit to Japan; the poem "Is
there no way out?" [¿No hay salida?] is written there. In 1954, a
long essay on *Genji, The Pillow Book,* Zen, Nō, and haiku. In 1955
the Mexican haiku of *Loose Stones* [Piedras sueltas] and the first

[1] *Tarde.* Leve piel de nube/donde anda clavada/la astilla de luna.

Western translation of Bashō's poetry and prose travel journal, *Sendas de Oku* [in Cid Corman's translation of the title, *Back Roads to Far Towns*], written with Eikichi Hayashiya. Erotic haiku in *Salamander* [Salamandra, 1962]. Throughout the 1960s and 1970s, translations of Chinese and Japanese poets. *East Slope* [Ladera este, 1969], arguably his best book of poetry, takes its title from the Sung Dynasty poet Su Shih, who wrote under the name Su Tung-p'o (East Slope). The pages on Taoism and Chinese eroticism in *Conjunctions and Disjunctions* [Conjunciones y disyunciones, 1969]. That same year, Paz collaborates with Charles Tomlinson, Eduardo Sanguineti, and Jacques Roubaud on the quadrilingual *Renga*. In 1970, a major essay, "The Tradition of the Haiku" in the second edition of the Bashō book (reprinted in English in *Convergences*). In the 1970s and 1980s, short essays on Tu Fu, Wang Wei, Han Yu, and other Chinese poets. In 1976, the Japanese translation of *The Labyrinth of Solitude*, the first of many Paz books to be translated into that language. In 1979, *Hijos del aire/Airborn*, a variation on renga written with Tomlinson. In 1984, a visit to Japan and pilgrimage to Bashō's hut. In 1989, Duo Duo, the young Chinese poet avidly read by the students demonstrating in Tiananmen Square, remarks that his favorite poet is Octavio Paz.

•

> *The god that emerges from an orchid of clay*
> Born smiling
> From ceramic petals:
> A human flower.[1]

Like the invention of *mole* in a convent in Puebla: the adaptation of Eastern techniques, employing indigenous Mexican materials, in an essentially Western context. The poem, from *Loose Stones*, is of course written in Spanish, and not Nahuatl or Japanese; its form is a loose haiku; its subject the tiny Jaina god—a god, by the

---

[1] *Dios que surge de una orquídea de barro.* Entre los petalos de arcilla / nace, sonriente, / la flor humana.

way, identical to the Apsarasas emerging from lotuses in the exactly contemporaneous T'ang art. A tropicalization of the haiku not invented by Paz—in the 1930s the Guatemalan Flavio Herrera was writing haiku like: "Happy/to be Indian, it smiles:/an ear of corn."[1]—but perfected by him.

What Paz, as so many others, found in the haiku was verbal concision, a precision based on close observation of the world, particularly the natural world, and the sense that a poem remains permanently at the verge of completion, never arriving, as Western art once attempted, at a finished totality. The reader always supplies the rest of a haiku, and it changes with each reading. The haiku is a tiny graph of relations within the natural world—a world that includes its human observers—but these relations, according to Buddhism, are as illusory as the interacting beings. For both poet and reader it is a sudden act of the discovery and affirmation of a comradeship in illusion.

1955 as a turning point in a work that keeps turning. In 1952, his one poem written in Japan, "Is there no way out?" begins, in Denise Levertov's translation, "Dozing I hear an incessant river running between dimly discerned, looming forms, drowsy and frowning."[2] The language, as in the other poems of this period, is lush, vague, rhetorical, Surrealist, unchained, interior. (Japan, of course, is notable for its absence of any major river.) After 1955 and his actual working with haiku—*Loose Stones* and the Bashō translation—Paz is able to bring the period to a close by joining the luxuriant rhetoric to a precise imagery that is far more concrete than anything previous in his or any one else's Surrealism: the incantatory *Sunstone* [Piedra de sol, 1957]:

> a crystal willow, a poplar of water,
> a tall fountain the wind arches over . . .[3]

[1] Feliz/de ser india, sonrie/la mazorca de maíz.
[2] En duermevela oigo correr entre bultos adormilados y ceñudos un incesante río.
[3] Un sauce de cristal, un chopo de agua,/un alto surtidor que el viento arquea . . .

And from
there, the almost inevitable move is toward an adaptation of
Pound's "ideogrammic method": the stepped lines, the free-
floating images forming configurations of meaning, the simultaneity of *Days and Occasions* [Días hábiles, 1961]:

> Night in the bones
> > skeleton night
> the headlights touch your secret plazas
> the sanctuary of the body
> > the ark of the spirit
> the lips of the wound
> > the wooded cleft of the oracles[1]

•

Four poets in four languages meet for five days to write a series
of collective poems. *Renga* (1969), the experiment, is an ideogram composed of many of Paz's essential elements:

The belief,
from Lautréamont, that in the future poetry will be composed by
the multitude, not the individual. The disappearance of the author, as it comes out of the Surrealist practices of automatic
writing and the game of "exquisite corpse," and—more recently
at the time—French structuralism. Buddhism's sublimation of
the ego as the first step toward the recognition of *sunyata*, emptiness. Hindu and Buddhist emphasis on relation rather than substance. The pluralism and multilingualism of the 20th century.
Translation as the creation of a third language somewhere between the "source" and the "target"; and equally, as the creation
of a third poet. A collaborative, quadrilingual poem as the expression of an era, rather than an author. The Western adaptation of a traditional Eastern form, applying some of its methods,
but few of its rules.

And yet *Renga,* the book, is a disappoint-

[1] Noche en los huesos / noche calavera / los reflectores palpan tus plazas se-
cretas / el sagrario del cuerpo / el arca del espíritu / los labios de la herida / la bos-
cosa hendidura de la profecía.

ment: the poems lack even the vivacity of the linked haiku collaboratively written by the Beats ten years before. Perhaps the problem is that *Renga* is not renga.

Renga is a chain: a three-line haiku by one poet, then two additional lines by the next to form a five-line tanka, then three more lines, added to the two above to form another tanka. Two discrete tanka out of eight lines: the end of one is the beginning of another. And so on forever, or until other more elaborate rules—refined over the centuries—declare the chain is over.

Renga is an endless series of permutations, changing over time. It is a game that is an image of the universe. But *Renga* is a group of 28 sonnets in four groups of seven; each author contributing a quatrain or tercet, and the entirety of one of the final sonnets. Unlike renga, the form is closed: the effect is that of four painters, each painting a quarter of 24 canvases (but, unlike the "exquisite corpse," aware of what the others are doing). Canvases that are painted simultaneously, four at a time: the process is visible, but the product is dominant.

Nor do the authors vanish: each is made visible by his language, though there is some leakage from one language to the other, and each is the sole author of one of the sonnets. (Sanguineti's sonnet, however, is silence.) And, stuck in a basement in a Paris hotel, instead of outside where renga is usually composed, the poems are filled with the interior bric-a-brac of four erudites observing, not the moon or the plum blossoms, but each other, writing.

A modern renga would be more like a multi-authored *Cantos:* its end could not be predicted from its beginning; it would often proceed by association; it would be a babble of unidentified voices (its authors, if multilingual, writing in each other's languages); its pace would be that of time-lapse cinematography, a single cell swiftly multiplying into hundreds of organisms; it would be abandoned rather than finished; it would be an emblem of restless change.

Since the mid-1950s Paz has continued to practice haiku and to learn, from Chinese poetry, to record the instantaneous moment in the natural world. Yet he has never indulged in Orientalism. One of his most "Chinese" poems, "Concord" (dedicated to Carlos Fuentes):

> Water above
> Grove below
> Wind on the roads
>
> Quiet well
> Bucket's black   Spring water
>
> Water coming down to the trees
> Sky rising to the lips[1]

takes its first two lines from the *I Ching* (the 28th hexagram, Ta Kuo: "The lake rises above the trees: The image of 'Preponderance of the Great.' Thus the superior man, when he stands alone, is unconcerned, and if he has to renounce the world, he is undaunted.") The poem's middle lines are an observed Indian landscape; its last line one of the most beautiful Surrealist images. And somewhere behind it all, as nearly always in Paz, a tiny piece of Mexico is transformed; in this case, a 1912 poem by Alfonso Reyes, "Cluster of Sky":

> Rage above:
> Calm below.
> Weathervanes rattle,
> the blinds weep.
>
> The celestial cattle slowly rise
> from the diaphanous courted sheep.[2]

---

[1] *Concorde.* Arriba el agua / abajo el bosque / el viento por los caminos // Quietud del pozo / El cubo es negro El agua firme // El agua baja hasta los árboles / El cielo sube hasta los labios.

[2] *Gajo de cielo.* Abajo, la rabia: / arriba, la calma. / Las veletas claman, / lloran las persianas. // Lentas ascienden las celestes vacas, / de diáfanos corderos cortejadas.

Idle speculations:

        Had Paz not discovered the disappearance of the author in automatic writing and renga, would he not have found it in the Nahuatl tradition, which does not distinguish between poet and poem, where a poet can declare: "God has sent me as a messenger. / I am transformed into a poem"? And had Pound not invented the "ideogrammic method," would not Paz have evolved a similar theory, based on the Maya glyph?

        The glyphs, after all, like Chinese characters, are conglomerates of component parts: simple pictographs (a jaguar for "jaguar"), phonetic signs (each representing a single syllable), logographs (non-representational representations of a word), and semantic determinatives (specifiers of particular meaning).

        For those who cannot read them—and this was articulated most notably by Charles Olson in the Yucatán in the 1950s—the glyphs have a concreteness, a weight, that does not exist in alphabetic writing: the word is an object. And more: it appears, to the outsider, that each glyph, each word, has the *same* weight. The glyph-covered stela becomes the ideal, irreducible, poem. Olson:

> What continues to hold me, is, the tremendous levy on all objects as they present themselves to human sense, in this glyph-world. And the proportion, the distribution of weight given same parts of all, seems, exceptionally, distributed & accurate, that is, that
> sun
>   moon
>   venus
>   other constellations & zodiac
> snakes
>   ticks
>   vultures
> jaguar
>   owl
>   frog
> feathers
>   peyote
>   water-lily

not to speak of
fish
        caracol
                tortoise
&, above all
human eyes
        hands
                limbs
                        PLUS EXCEEDINGLY CAREFUL OBSERVA-
                        TION OF ALL POSSIBLE INTERVALS OF
                        SAME . . .
And the weights of same, each to the other, is, immaculate (as well as,
full)

For those who can read them—as has become increasingly
possible—the glyphs become even more like poetry, for each
word could be represented in pictographic, geometric, or syllabic
form (which corresponds to Pound's *phanopoeia, logopoeia,* and
melopoeia). There are seemingly unlimited ways to represent any
given word, and the continual invention of glyphs was a dazzling
display of association, homophony, and punning. Laid out in a
grid, these metamorphosing word-clusters could be read in a
variety of ways, both horizontally and vertically. The Maya
"text," as far as we now know, was a net of continually changing
correspondences, and reading an intricate game for skilled
players.

There is a line from Palenque to "Blanco" that does not
pass through Mallarmé.

4. The figure is the landscape

As an adolescent, Octavio Paz discovers Anglo-American Mod-
ernism in *The Waste Land.* First visit to India in 1952; the poem
"Mutra" is written there. From 1962 to 1968, Ambassador to
India. Meets and marries Marie-José Tramini. The poems of
East Slope, including "Blanco." The essays on Buddhist logic,

Hinduism, caste, published in *Alternating Current* [Corriente
alterna, 1967]. In 1969, his major meditation on East and West,
Conjunctions and Disjunctions. In 1970, Paz organizes the first
exhibition of Tantric art in the West, at the Galerie Le Point
Cardinal in Paris; the catalog contains the important essay
"Blank Thought" [El pensamiento en blanco]. The same year he
writes his "unraveling novel" of a pilgrimage to Galta in Rajasthan, *The Monkey Grammarian* [El mono gramático]. In the
1970s and 1980s, although there are no major poems or essays
dealing specifically with India, references, particularly to Buddhism and Tantrism, are made throughout. In 1985 Paz revisits
India.

The god Vishnu appears at the cave of an ascetic, Narada, who
has been practicing austerities for decades. Narada asks the god
to teach him about the power of *maya,* illusion. The god beckons
Narada to follow him. They find themselves in the middle of a
burning desert. Vishnu tells Narada he is thirsty, and asks him to
fetch some water from a village he will find on the other side of
the hill. Narada runs to the village and knocks at the first door,
which is opened by a beautiful young woman. He stares at her
and forgets why he has come. He enters the house; her parents
treat him with respect; the following year they are married. He
lives in the joys of marriage and the hardships of village life.
Twelve years go by: they have three children; his father-in-law
has died and Narada has inherited the small farm. That year,
a particularly fierce monsoon brings floods: the cattle are
drowned, their house collapses. Carrying his children, they
struggle through the water. The smallest child slips away. He
puts the two children down to search for her; it is too late. As he
returns he sees the other two children swept off; his wife, swimming after them, is pulled under. A branch strikes Narada on the
head; he is knocked unconscious and carried along. When he
awakes he finds himself on a rock, sobbing. Suddenly he hears a
voice: "My child! Where's that water you were bringing me? I've
been waiting nearly half an hour." Narada opens his eyes and
finds himself alone with Vishnu on the burning desert plain.

Is this not the "plot" of the first two sections of *East Slope?*

The book opens with the lines "Stillness/in the middle of the night"[1]—the poet is alone on a balcony overlooking Old Delhi—and then it immediately fills, overflows, with Indian stuff: monuments, landscapes, a jungle of specific flora and fauna, painters, musicians, gardens, gods, palaces, tombs, philosophy, temples, history, bits of Indian English, a large cast of strange and funny characters—the only characters in Paz's poetry—and, central to it all, the lover/wife. In the end, in "A Tale of Two Gardens" [Cuento de dos jardines], it all vanishes: "The garden sinks./ Now it is a name with no substance. // The signs are erased: / I watch clarity."[2] The poet is not in the desert, but in the middle of the equally empty ocean on a boat leaving India. (Although—this being poetry and not philosophy—his wife, rather than Vishnu, is with him.)

Maya is made manifest by time. The Indian cosmos is a map of ever-widening concentric cycles of enormous time: millions of human years with their perpetual reincarnations are merely one day and night in the millions of years in the life of Brahma, who is himself but one incarnation in an endless succession of Brahmas. The function of yoga and other meditation practices is to break out of these cycles of illusory births and rebirths, off the map (out of the calendar) and into the undifferentiated bliss of *nirvana* (which the Buddhists would later say was equally illusory).

Myth is a similar rupture of time. Its time is intemporal time, and though its narration unfolds in measured minutes and hours it abolishes time with its narration. Narrator and auditor are projected into a sacred space from which they view historical time and all its products: a world to which they must return, but to which they return educated.

The poem too, though heard in a time that has its own precise mea-

[1] Quieta / en mitad de la noche.
[2] El jardín se abisma. / Ya es un nombre sin substancia. // Los signos se borran: / yo miro la claridad.

surements (prosody), erases time by projecting us into a world
where everything looks the same but is more vivid, where we
speak the language but it doesn't sound like the language we
speak, where ideas and emotions become concrete particulars,
and the concrete is a manifestation of the divine.

The first two sections ("East Slope" and "Toward the Beginning") of *East Slope* are "travel poetry": a poetry of verifiable
landscapes, things and people which are foreign to the author.
But they are among the few instances in the last two hundred
years of a travel poetry worth reading. (Poets, since the birth of
Romanticism, have tended to write their travels in prose and
letters.) One reason is its precision of observation, its glittering
language, intellectual cadenzas, emotional and erotic rhapsodies.
But more: on nearly every page are synonyms of silence and
stillness. The poems are simultaneously located in India and in a
not-India, a somewhere else.

As Aztec shamans would travel out
of the earth to a place where all time was visible in a state of total
immobility. There they could observe the life-force of the *tonalli*
at any given moment before it occurred in human life. The
shaman's task was to alter the tonalli, to effectively rewrite the
future.

As the first two sections of *East Slope* observe the world
from a world where the wind comes simultaneously from everywhere, where "the present is perpetual" and bodies "weigh no
more than the dawn."

Paz, above all, is a religious poet whose
religion is poetry. This does not mean that the poet is a "little
God," as Huidobro dreamed, with extraordinary powers. Rather
it is the poem that opens a hairline crack in time through which
the poet, in astonishment, slips through.

The final third of *East Slope*—the long poem "Blanco"—is both
the most "Indian" poem in the book, and the one with the fewest
images of India. (In fact, only three words in the poem pertain
specifically to India: the *neem* tree and the musical instruments
sitar and *tabla*. Only three more refer to phenomena that exist in

India and other places, but are not universal: *crow, jasmine, vulture.*)

The form of the poem, originally published on a single vertical folded sheet in black and red type—"black and red ink" in Nahuatl means "wisdom"—is usually described as a hybrid descended from Mallarmé's *Un Coup de des* . . . and Indo-Tibetan mandalas. Neither is accurate. Mallarmé's poem, though it plays with varying typefaces and blank space, still uses a traditional (though oversize) page as its playing field: it exists to end up in a book. It is more likely that the Western grandparent of "Blanco" is the original 1913 edition, designed by Sonia Delaunay, of Cendrar's "Prose of the Transsiberian." It too is a floor-to-ceiling vertical sheet with different typefaces in black and red, but unlike "Blanco" the words are not surrounded by emptiness: every inch is covered with Delaunay's hallucinogenic color, itself a kind of Indian festival.

On the Eastern side, the poem is not really a mandala, although it has been described by Paz as such: mandalas are complex configurations of circles within squares, filled with iconic images of the gods. "Blanco" of course has no gods, other than poetry, and its representational imagery tends to be abstract. The poem, rather, is more like the yogic and tantric vertical scrolls depicting the ascent of the *kundalini* (the "serpent power" of latent energy). Such scrolls represent the human body, though an outline of the body itself is rarely shown. From bottom to top are images of the seven *chakras,* the energy centers that run from the base of the spine to the top of the head, and through which the kundalini ascends during yogic meditation or tantric practice. Each of the chakras has a host of attributes: elements, colors, senses, planets, emotions, philosophical concepts, and so on.

"Blanco," which must necessarily be read down the page (it not being written in Maya) can be seen, loosely, as an upside-down diagram of the chakras. Its first two vertical sections (before it splits into left and right) correspond to the first chakra at the base of the spine, Muladhara, which means "the foundation" (the first two lines of the poem are: *"el comienzo/ el cimiento"* or "the beginning/ the foundation") and which is associated with the *bija,* the syllable-seed (the next two lines are: *"la simiente / latente"* or "the seed / latent") from which all sound, all language, and everything in the cosmos is born. Other attributes of the Muladhara chakra are the earth (*"escalera de escapulario"*—an earth-body pun meaning both "mineshaft/scapulary ladder") and the color yellow (which appears in "Blanco" as the "yellow chalice of consonants and vowels").[1]

From there the kundalini rises as the poem descends through the other chakras—though not strictly: most of the attributes of the chakras are present in "Blanco," though not quite in the same order. It never reaches the final, seventh chakra, the illumination of the void: to do so, in a poem, would be less presumptuous than impossible: at that point poetry ceases to be written. But it does, following this schema, reach the sixth, called Ajna ("power"). That is the point between the eyebrows (the last word of the poem is *mirada,* "gaze"), where all the elements return in purified form (as they do in the poem), and whose "color" is transparency ("transparency is all that remains").[2] Its reigning god is Ardhanarishvara, who is the half-male, half-female incarnation of Shiva, the union of all opposites ("No and yes" and the many other pairs which unite in this section of the poem). And it is associated with *nada,* cosmic sound, which becomes a complex Spanish-Sanskrit pun in "Blanco": *"son palabras/ aire son nada"* (with *son* meaning both "sound" and "they are"; *nada* both "nothing" and "cosmic sound"): "sound (they are) words/ air sound (they are) nothing (cosmic sound)." The seed-syllables, though made of air, form words, form the cosmic sound, form the universe. The three are inextricable, and equally illusory: Sanskrit *nada* is Spanish *nada.* (There is a form of meditation, rather like "Blanco," called *nada-yoga,* which consists of focusing on a succession of sounds as they emerge from and retreat into silence.)

[1] Amarillo/ cáliz de consonantes y vocales.
[2] La transparencia es todo lo que queda.

Further, in this map of the Hindu body and of "Blanco," there are three "nerves" or "veins" which convey sacred breath and the body's subtle energies. The left, *lalana,* is feminine and associated with the moon, wisdom, emptiness, nature, the Ganges River, vowels. The right, *rasana,* is masculine and associated with the sun, intellect, compassion, method, the Yamuna (the other great river in India), consonants. In the center is *avadhuti,* the union of the two veins and all their attributes. Again, a schema followed loosely in the poem through its left, right, and center columns.

The map of the body is a map of the earth is a map of the cosmos (or time) is a map of language. Most of Paz's work is, and has always been, concerned with the tangle of correspondences among these four elements, their identicalness, their transformations into one another. He is surely Western poetry's primary "inventor of India for our time" (as Eliot called Pound the inventor of China); but he is equally an invention of India: "Indian" readings are possible for poems he wrote long before he went there.

Much has been written about the connections between "Blanco" and the ritual copulation practiced in Tantrism: an escape from the world (and a return to the original unity of the world) through the union of all opposites as incarnated in the actual bodies of the male and female adepts. (The best texts on this are still Paz's pages in *Conjunctions and Disjunctions* and the essay "Blank Thought.")

Robert Duncan, in the era of "action painting" in the 1950s, used to emphasize that the poem "is not the record of the event, but the event itself." "Blanco," though far too structured to be an "event" of writing in the processual sense developed by the Black Mountain poets, demands reader participation in the creation of the text by offering a list of variant readings that is, moreover, deliberately left incomplete. Writer and reader are yet another pair of opposites who unite in the poem. But "Blanco" goes even further: with its male center column and female split columns, it is, uniquely in erotic poetry, a poem that makes love to itself. (As, in India, the syllable-seeds engender language without human assistance.) The author has closed the door behind him on his way out; like Duchamp's *Etant donnés,* it remains for the reader to peer (or not) through the keyhole.

Tantric texts are written in *sandha,* which Mircea Eliade translates as "intentional" language. Each word carries a long string of associative possibilities, like those attributed to the three yogic "veins" above: the spiritual words have materialist and erotic meanings, and vice-versa. (The "right-hand" group of Tantrists believes that all of the material words should be taken only as metaphors for the spiritual; the "left-hand" group believes that all of the spiritual words are merely code names for aspects of the rituals, which, like copulation on a cremation ground, are scandalous to outsiders.)

There is a pair of sandha-words in the *Hevajra Tantra* (a line of which Paz rewrites as an epigraph to "Blanco") that is particularly intriguing: *preksana* (the act of seeing) is *agati* (the act of arrival or achievement). In India the primary act of daily worship among Hindus is *darshana* (seeing): it is both a "viewing" of the gods as they are manifest in the temple and wayside images, and something more: in darshana the eyes literally touch the gods; sight goes out to physically receive the god's blessing.

"Blanco" ends at the chakra between the eyes. Its last line reiterates an earlier couplet ("The unreality of the seen/brings reality to seeing")[1] in the context of a ritualized copulation: "Your body/spilled on my body/seen/dissolved/brings reality to seeing."[2] The poem, then, never erases the world, never enters the "plentiful void" of nirvana (as the last canto of *Altazor* does: a void filled with syllable-seeds) or the "empty void" of sunyata. In the unreality of the world the poem

---

[1] La irrealidad de lo mirado/da realidad a la mirada.

[2] Tu cuerpo/derramado en mi cuerpo/visto/desvanecido/da realidad a la mirada.

ends by affirming the reality of a seeing which is touching which is writing.

Tantric art is notable for its representation of the cosmos in a simple or complex geometric drawing: the *yantra*. Paz's India (India's Paz) is a yantra composed of a triangle (seeing-touching-writing) within a square (body-world-cosmos-language) within a circle, which in India stands for a vision or a system. An O that is a poet's political button, this poet's monogram, and the egg (symbol and syllable) of the cosmos.

In the meditation, the yogin imagines a lotus blossoming on his navel. On the petals of the lotus are the letters of the mantra ARHAN. Smoke appears, rising from the letter R. Suddenly a spark, a burst of flame, and the lotus is consumed by fire. The wind picks up and scatters the ashes, covering him from head to toe. Then a gentle rain falls, and slowly washes them away. Bathed, refreshed, the yogin sees his body shining like the moon.

[1990]

THE DESERT MUSIC

There are a few things we know for certain about the Nazca lines, and the first is their immensity. Covering 85 square miles of a rainless moonscape in southern Peru, Nazca is a palimpsest, an unerased blackboard filled with straight lines and spirals; vast trapezoids, rectangles, and truncated triangles; and, in one corner of the plain, huge figures of birds, fish, monkeys, whales, insects, flowers. There are six hundred miles of lines that are still visible; originally there may have been twice as many. The longest is 4½ miles long; the average length is a mile. The largest figure alone covers 37 acres.

They were created by breaking up and sweeping away the "desert varnish," a dark oxidized crust, to reveal the lighter stone beneath. In this fashion some 1,600 acres were cleared, 2,000 to 1,000 years ago, by a culture or cultures now called Nasca (with an "s") of which not much else remains.

The Spanish never noticed the lines. They were rediscovered in the 1920s when planes began flying from Peru to Chile, and ever since it has been assumed that they are best seen—moreover, were meant to be seen—from the air. In the early 1970s they entered popular consciousness through a bestseller, *Chariots of the Gods,* which maintained that nearly all the human accomplishments of the remote past were performed or directed by extraterrestrials. The Nazca figures were for summoning spaceships, and the lines were airport runways—though why a spaceship would need a runway was hardly explained.

There have been, of course, more scholarly readings of the lines, some of them equally weird, nearly all of them a mirror of self-interest. Astronomers and archeo-astronomers have believed that the lines are strictly celestially oriented. Alexander Thom, an engineer famous for his work at Stonehenge, saw them primarily as a massive feat of engineering. Maria Reiche, a

German mathematician who arrived in 1932 and has been self-appointed guardian of the plain ever since—that strange phenomenon of the single European woman who takes over a particular archeological site or tribal group: "Om Seti" in Luxor or Gertrude Blom among the Lacandóns of Chiapas—believes that the zoomorphic figures contain an esoteric geometry; hers are similar to theories about the Great Pyramid at Giza. One archeologist thought the lines were running tracks for an Andean Olympics, complete with team shirts and headgear he found represented on the pottery. Another saw them as a huge WPA-style make-work project in a time of economic decline. Others believed the plain was a burial ground and a site for ceremonies honoring the dead. In the 1970s, "earthworks" artists like Robert Morris claimed Nazca as a kindred ancestral project and considered it the product of purely aesthetic acts.

For the last ten years, some of the best archeologists and ethnographers of Latin America—including Anthony Aveni, Gary Urton, and R. T. Zuidema—have been working in Nazca. They have not only taken the first complete survey of the plain; they've walked most of the lines. And they have based their speculations on two undeniably sensible assumptions: First, that there were no spaceships or pre-Columbian aircraft; the lines were meant to be seen from the ground or the adjoining hills. Second, that what we know of other Andean cultures—the Inkas, who were described in detail by the early conquistadors, as well as contemporary groups—may be helpful in understanding the Nascas. Their conclusions, however tentative, are as remarkable as any of the earlier theories.

The river valleys that border Nazca have been inhabited for millennia, but no one has ever lived on the plain itself. For at least a thousand years it was purely a sacred space reserved for ceremonial occasions. [And as a sacred space, it may be unique: unlike the caves or kivas leading into the underworld; the stupas which defined a space that could not be entered, but only circled; or the churches, pyramids, and temples that reached to the sky— Nazca was a two-dimensional space, an horizon between the gods of the earth and sky.] The nature of those ceremonies apparently changed: the animal and plant figures are much earlier, possibly the works of another culture; the lines are the traces of a far more sophisticated society.

The lines themselves, Aveni has discovered, have an arrangement: nearly all are connected to 62 radiating centers. A few of them are indeed astronomical, pointing to the sun at the solstices, the bright stars Alpha and Beta Centauri (which the Inkas called "Eyes of the Llama"), the Southern Cross, and the Pleiades (which were a "storehouse"). More important, all of the radiating centers are near water, and the line directions match the orientations of the local streams. In the middle of the plain, at a place where water suddenly emerges from the ground, the Nascans built a city used only for pilgrimages and abandoned the rest of the year. Its name was Cahuachi; in Quechua *qhawachi* means "make them see."

What the people, and perhaps the gods above and below, were meant to see was a map of their world. There seems no doubt that the radiating centers are related to the *ceque* system, practiced by the Inkas, first described by Pedro de Cieza de León, a foot soldier who arrived in Peru fifteen years after Pizarro, and recently decoded by Zuidema. The Inkas, like many cultures, considered themselves the center of the universe: their name for their country, as is common elsewhere, was the Land of the Four Quarters, *Tawantinsuyu*. But unlike other cultures, the Inkas devised a complex cosmic and social organization based on that centrality. From the Temple of the Sun in their capital, Cuzco, 41 *ceques*—perfectly straight lines that ignored geographical obstacles—radiated. These lines, among the things we know, were pointed to astronomical phenomena as a kind of horizon calendar, divided the city according to various social and kinship groups, apportioned water rights, and—the comparison to the Songlines of the Australian Aborigines is inescapable—traced the history of the descent of rulership from the gods down through the Inka kings, and may have contained other stories.

Furthermore, the 41 ceque lines were punctuated by 328 *huacas:* sacred markers that were natural (caves, mountain tops, streams) or artificial (piles of stones, tombs, temples). This combination of lines and markers directly relates to one of the forms of Inka writing: the *quipu*. Quipus—of which only 400 survive— were a series of strings either suspended from a piece of wood, or radiating from a loop of thicker rope. These strings were twined countless ways in hundreds of colors; each string was marked with knots along its length. All of this could be read. Not only were the quipus used for inventories, accounts, and censuses—somewhere between an abacus and a calculator—they were a complete writing system, a repository for songs and history. Quechua itself, the language of the Andes, derives from *q'eswa,* meaning a rope.

[In a very early commentary on the *I Ching* there is a curious line: "In primitive times, people knotted cords to govern." And a 2nd century Chinese tomb has a relief of the ancestor-god Fu-Hsi and his sister-consort Nu-Kua holding a carpenter's square and a personified quipu. The inscription reads: "Dragon-bodied Fu Hsi first established kingly rule, drew the eight trigrams, and devised the knotted cords in order to govern all within the four seas." No ancient Chinese quipus have ever been discovered, but a rudimentary version was, until recently, used by the Miao tribe in the southwest of the country.]

Cuzco, then, was organized as a giant quipu, with the huacas as its knots. And so, quite probably, was Nazca. All of its lines are similarly marked by huacas: in this case, cairns (flat stones piled three feet high) or geographical features. Nazca was certainly a diagram: it may well have been a text. [It should be remembered that in South America the iconography of their gods and, most probably, their writing system were *geometric:* the Inkan woven *t'okapus* and wooden *keros,* checkerboards filled with complex patterns which the early Spanish chroniclers said were kept in libraries; or the intricate designs of Amazonian baskets that even today are narratives and songs.] The imperial city, then, literally contained, and was organized by, its own description: it was ruled by writing. The sacred plain, empty of the forms of life, was pure description itself: the world turned into writing. The plain was a page, the most mysterious of the sacred places.

What ceremonies occurred there? First, the act of making the lines, a sacred function which was probably divided according to the social groups—there are parallels to contemporary Andean practice—who may then have gathered for further rites in the newly swept "plazas" of the rectangles and trapezoids. Second, a ritual smashing of pottery—the plain is strewn with shards—like the potlatch ceremonies everywhere in the Americas: the assertion of power through the destruction of one's own property. Third—and again there are parallels to Inkan and contemporary practices—a ritual walking, running, or dancing down the lines. (Even the zoomorphic figures are composed of a single continuous line which never crosses itself, suggesting that it was meant to be traveled, a "way" to be followed. One entered, in the early centuries, the whaleness of the whale by walking the whale.)

No one was buried there. The lines, though they may have contained history or honored the dead, were an assertion, perhaps a celebration, of the known world. For the later Nascans, they were a sacred walk through the way things are: the flow of water and the flow of time, the hierarchy of social groups and the apportioning and maintenance of irrigation rights and agricultural stores, the gods watching from above and sending water from below, the movement of the stars, the ancient lineages, perhaps language itself. And they were an homage to the unknown world: many of the lines continue beyond visibility from their starting-point, and it is significant that no line points to the most prominent feature on the plain: a mountain, still sacred, called Cerro Blanco. The mountain, in the language of Nazca, was a word that could not be spoken.

That there are so many radiating centers on the plain is probably because different ones pertained to, and were used in, different years. Over time, the light stones darken again with the desert varnish; but the mere act of walking or dancing on the lines would have refreshed them, made them bright again. As William Carlos Williams said, a new line is a new mind.

[1991]

James Jesus Angleton 1917–1987

On his strange mission to America in 1939 to persuade Roosevelt not to enter the European war, Ezra Pound took time from his meetings with low-level bureaucrats and high-level avant-gardists to travel to New Haven to visit a Yale student named Jim Angleton. Angleton, still an undergraduate, was an energetic *littérateur*. He had visited Pound in Rapallo, and shared his enthusiasm for Mussolini. He was chummy with Cummings, met Marianne Moore, lunched with Thomas Mann, and had brought in the ambiguous William Empson to lecture; he helped James Agee with the manuscript of *Let Us Now Praise Famous Men*. Now, with his roommate Reed Whittemore, he was editing a poetry magazine called *Furioso*. Pound's one-page "Introductory Textbook" had appeared in the first number, and the poet was as eager as ever to tell the young editors whom to publish.

Details of that encounter are not known: the two major Pound biographies grant the incident only one, nearly identical sentence each. After four issues, *Furioso* suspended publication, to be resumed after the war with Whittemore as sole editor. Angleton was published only once, in the *Yale Literary Magazine*: a bad poem with a prophetic title, "The Immaculate Conversion." In the middle of the war, Angleton was converted— "turned," he would say—by his English professor, Norman Holmes Pearson, from poetry to its twin, espionage.

Pearson, a Boston aristocrat and a diminutive cripple, is now remembered for his writings on 19th-century American literature, the extraordinary *Poets of the English Language* anthologies he edited with W. H. Auden, and as H.D.'s editor and literary executor. In 1943, despite the fact that he had been a Nazi sympathizer until the invasion of Poland, Pearson was sent to London to become the head of X-2, the counter-intelligence branch of the O.S.S. (Office of Strategic Services). There he learned the British "Double Cross" system of psychologically coercing captured enemy agents into working for one's own side. Pearson's counterpart (and nemesis) at the British M.I.6 was Kim Philby; his code name was Puritan; in espionage literature he is called "the father of American counter-intelligence."

Angleton turned out to be Pearson's greatest find. Their relationship during the war was close: father-son, or master-disciple. After work at the London O.S.S. office, Angleton traveled in the Pearson circle: Eliot, the Sitwells, Benjamin Britten, Graham Greene, E. M. Forster, Ralph Vaughan Williams, Norman Douglas, Elizabeth Bowen, Compton MacKenzie. He was a frequent guest at H.D. and Bryher's flat.

The O.S.S. office itself was no less literary. Angleton had, in turn, recruited two close friends: Edward Weismiller, the Yale Younger Poet of 1936, and Richard Ellmann, the future Joyce scholar. Textual critics and Elizabethan scholars—many of them from Yale, and nearly all Ivy Leaguers—played the Great Game with fledgling superspooks like William Casey, who would later become Ronald Reagan's sphinx at the C.I.A. Angleton's secretary was H.D.'s daughter Perdita. (H.D. seems to have been surrounded by spies. It is curious that Bryher was apparently the only outside person to know Pearson's code name.)

After the war, Pearson returned to Yale, where he continued to recruit students for the newly formed C.I.A. He served on the board of advisers to Pound's Square Dollar Books, which folded after its publishers, John Kasper and Thomas Horton, went to jail for instigating segregationist riots. In 1975, on a tour of the Far East, Norman Holmes Pearson fell ill in Seoul and died soon after. Mrs. Pearson believed that he had been poisoned by North Koreans—proof that he was still working for the Company.

Angleton, when he surfaced in public in the late 1970s, was revealed to be the chief of C.I.A. counter-intelligence, the "ultra top secret deep snow" unit. He was noted for his deathly pallor, his chain-smoking, cryptic allusions to conspiracies, and his office piled with papers, the windows never opened and the curtains never drawn. He had files on two million Americans; had directed an operation that infiltrated the U.S. Postal Service and opened and photographed 200,000 personal letters; believed that Lee Harvey Oswald and Henry Kissinger were KGB spies, and that the Black Panthers were a North Korean front operation. He had been Kim Philby's best friend. For twenty years after the defection of Philby's partners Guy Burgess and Donald MacLean, Philby and Angleton were locked in a "deep game" of double and double-double crossing—a "wilderness of mirrors," Angleton called it, quoting Eliot—as Angleton decimated the ranks of the C.I.A. in search of double agents, the "moles." Angleton's boss, Allen Dulles, was kept uninformed, and Mrs. Angleton, after 31 years of marriage, had never known her husband's position.

Angleton, who kept reading poetry all his life, claimed in later years that he had always tried to recruit agents from the Yale English Department. He believed that those trained in the New Criticism, with its seven types of ambiguity, were particularly suited to the interpretation of intelligence data.

Consider, after all, the ways a spy's message may be read:

1) It is written by a loyal agent and its information is accurate.

2) It is written by a loyal agent but its information is only partially accurate.

3) It is written by a loyal agent but its information is entirely inaccurate.

4) It is written by a double agent and its information is completely false.

5) It is written by a double agent but its information is partially true, so that the false parts will be believed.

6) It is written by a double agent but its information is entirely true, so that the allegiance of the agent will not be discovered.

Moreover, the message is written in code, and liable to the vagaries of translation. And it is written in a highly condensed language, whose meanings can offer varying interpretations. Like a poem, the message is only as good as its reader. Roosevelt refused to believe a report on the imminent invasion of Pearl

Harbor; the F.B.I. thought that *The Pisan Cantos* were the encoded communications of a spy.

There is a book to be written on poetry and espionage. A spy must know where the best information is, collect it without being discovered, and safely transmit it. In antiquity, the bards and troubadours were perfect for the task: they were free to wander; they had access to the courts; and as poets they relied on their powers of observation to compose and their memories to recite. The first literary spy is the creation of such a bard: Odysseus, who (in Book IV of the *Odyssey*) disguises himself as a beggar to gather intelligence in a Trojan city.

Chaucer was a spy on the continent for John of Gaunt. Marlowe was recruited by Sir Francis Walsingham—Elizabeth's great spymaster and Sir Philip Sidney's father-in-law—to inform on English students who were enjoying Catholic hospitality in Rheims. (And later, Marlowe was murdered by Walsingham's men because of his involvement with Sir Walter Ralegh, another spy, in a plot to depose the queen—a murder that was neatly staged to look like a barroom brawl.) Wordsworth was a spy in France; Basil Bunting a spy in Persia. Whittaker Chambers started out as an Objectivist poet and Louis Zukofsky's best friend.

Split between the power of the poem and the powerlessness of the poet in society, poets have lived the lives of spies. They have believed they are the "unacknowledged legislators," a secret police. They have been attracted to secret societies, from the Elizabethan School of Night (Ralegh, Spenser, Chapman, and Marlowe, as well as the alchemist Walter Warner) to Yeats' Golden Dawn. They have preferred to publish anonymously or under pseudonyms. They have been—like Milton writing his elegy before he had a suitable corpse—masters at the counterfeiting of emotions. They have banded together into groups and movements that, like Angleton's C.I.A., become obsessed with betrayals from within. They have encoded private messages and secret strengths into their poems. They have believed they are serving great powers: Stalin, Mussolini, the Revolution, the Church. They have walked, like Baudelaire, Lorca, Reznikoff, invisibly through the city, watching and listening. They have sat alone in their rooms, imagining the great plots unfolding outside.

Writes Mina Loy: "To maintain my incognito the hazard I chose was—poet." In its obituary, *The New York Times* reported that Angleton's favorite poets were Eliot and Cummings.

[1987]

3 NOTES ON POETRY

1. "Everything 'dead' trembles,"

writes Wassily Kandinsky in 1913: "Not only the stars, moon, wood and flowers of which the poets sing, but also a cigarette butt lying in an ashtray, a patient white trouser button looking up from a puddle in the street . . . everything shows me its face, its innermost being, its secret soul."

At the same moment, the other K of the Russian avant-garde, Velimir Khlebnikov is writing: "The only freedom we demand is freedom from the dead."

The modernist project of exalting the new and obliterating the rest, of replacing sunflowers with spark plugs as inspirational source and imaginative subject, aged faster than the gadgets of its affection. But the opposite drift of the modern—the recovery of everything, the inclusion of all that had been excluded—remains vivid, for the continuing lesson of the century is the sameness of the stuff of the world:

Trouser buttons may have turned to zippers, but both, like stars and wood, became recognized as merely varying configurations of the same subatomic particles. People were discovered to have the same dreams, tell the same stories, construct variants of the same societies. The same genetic rules were applied to clams and conquerors.

In this brotherhood (sisterhood) of the same, everything takes on an equal weight: Lautréamont's umbrella and sewing machine meet (make love) on the dissecting table. And what they produce—say, a trouser button—becomes as worthy an object of contemplation as an Alpine sunrise or the ruins of Karnak.

There's a story that George Washington Carver had a dream. God appeared before him, and told Carver to ask anything he wanted to know. Carver said, "Tell me everything about the peanut." God replied: "Your mind is too small to understand a peanut."

The modernist enthusiasm for archaic art was not merely a developing taste for simple forms and complex assemblages, as the current history runs. What the Moderns saw were manifestations of power. These strange or common objects were made to control life and death, sex and weather and food and illness. They were meant to change their world.

And in that universe of identical things—theirs and now ours—what is not the same, what remains in a state of continual change, is the relation among the things. The same particles spin into hawk and mouse, Anthony and Cleopatra, paint and canvas, Abbott and Costello: the world begins when they collide.

But more: switch them around and it's a different world: mouse and canvas, Abbott and Cleopatra . . .

(Or Cleopatra and her nose. Pascal ruminates: If it had been longer, the face of the world would have changed.)

In the luminous net of relations the slightest change—even watching—changes it all. To cut a single fern frond and stick it in the middle of a trail. The gesture would be meaningless, except in New Guinea, among the Kaluli, where it means that the souls of the bananas will not escape from a newly planted field: there'll be food.

Magic is dependent on the power latent in the least conspicuous object. A few fingernail parings can kill a man; a feather can ward off a hurricane. It is the context, and the act of placing in the context, that gives the useless scrap its power.

And what happens when that act occurs

outside of its culture—or more exactly, occurs in a culture that does not automatically recognize its significance? What happens, in other words, when Schwitters picks a bus ticket out of a Berlin gutter and pastes it on a canvas alongside of similar debris?

As an act of magic, it belongs to a private superstition: a charm in someone else's pocket. And yet a Schwitters bus ticket is strangely numinous: that representation of a world by its most insignificant member remains far more moving than the contemporary celebrations of dirigibles and hydroelectric plants.

It is a Chinese wisdom: the grass bends under the conquering armies; when they have swept by, it stands up again. The particular is epic.

And poetry, all poetry, is an epic of particulars arrayed on a limitless grid of information. Not only in erudite high modernism where, to take its most famous example, *The Waste Land,* one cannot speak of the supposed emptiness of modern life without reference to Grail legends and the sermons of the Buddha. To start anywhere, with any poem, is to enter the histories, mythologies, philosophies, topographies . . . the encyclopedic shelves of books that have informed or that might inform each line.

In countless oral stories the hunter, tracking a certain prey, follows an unrepeatable path into another world. It is the origin of the "way," in its universal religious sense. Poetry's "way"— both for its readers and its writers—is the lifetime (lifetimes) of intellectual and physical wanderings on the track of poems.

Everything living and dead trembles: their vibrations, like radio waves, are everywhere, go everywhere. Not only a chart of those wave patterns, not only an antenna for picking up the news and music, poetry is a homing device: a way through the zillion bits of the world to be learned from what is traditionally considered to be the most rarefied, unworldly world of writing.

[1990]

2. Translating

I've said it before: Poetry is that which is worth translating. The poem dies when it has no place to go.

The object of a translation into English is not a poem in English.

A translation creates a specific kind of distance ("willing suspension"): the reader never forgets that what is being read is a translation.

A translation that sounds like a poem in English is usually a bad translation.

A translation that strives for the accuracy of a bilingual dictionary is always a bad translation.

A translation must sound like a translation written in living English—and more, an English that takes advantage of certain possibilities that are not normally available to poems written in English.

The success of a translation is nearly always dependent on the smallest words: prepositions, articles. Anyone can translate nouns.

A foreign word with multiple meanings can—though few do it—be translated into several English words. One word can lead to a few, just as a few words can lead to one.

Effects that cannot be reproduced in the corresponding line can usually be picked up elsewhere, and should be. Which is why it is more difficult to translate a single poem than a book of poems by a single author. Which is why a translation shouldn't be, though it always is, judged on a line-by-line basis.

Few translators hear what they've written.

Pound intuitively corrected mistakes in the Fenollosa manuscript. For the rest of us, it is almost impossible to translate from a language one doesn't know. To translate through an "informant" is to paint by numbers: it's their design, you merely add some color.

Everything can be translated. That which is "untranslatable" hasn't yet found its translator.

The original is never better than the translation. The translation is worse than another translation, written or not yet written, of the same original.

Translation is not duplication. Every reading is a new reading: why should we expect a translation to be identical?

Metaphor: from the familiar to the strange. Translation: from the strange to the familiar. The failed metaphor is too strange; the failed translation too familiar.

Many of the best translators know the original language imperfectly. All of the worst translators are native speakers of it.

Translations are normally reviewed by members of the Department of the original's Language. They are proprietary, and cannot help but find all translations from their language—except those done by certain colleagues—to be travesties.

Translation theory, however beautiful, is useless for translating. There are the laws of thermodynamics, and there is cooking.

Most translators are capable of translating only a few writers in their lifetimes. The rest is rote.

A translation is based on the dissolution of the self. A bad translation is the insistent voice of the translator.

To translate is to learn how poetry is written. Nothing else is so successful a teacher, for it carries no baggage of self-expression.

Any poem should be translated as many times as possible, even by the same translator over the years. Only fundamentalists believe in a "definitive" translation.

A translation of classical Greek from 1900, say, is "dated" in a way that an English poem from 1900 is not, for we expect a translation to be written in a version of current speech, and refuse to make the mental readjustments as we would for a contemporaneous poem. With greater time, however—say, an Elizabethan translation from the classical Greek—such recalibration becomes inescapable: the translation, in our reading, becomes part of the age in which it was written.

Nearly everywhere, the great ages of poetry have been, not coincidentally, periods of intense translation. With no news from abroad, a culture ends up repeating the same things to itself. It needs the foreign not to imitate, but to transform.

An anonymous occupation, yet people have died for it.

[1988]

3. Believing

Fascism, Nazism, Communism are inextricable from much of the poetry of this, the most barbaric of the centuries. They arose in response to that new phenomenon of the 19th century: mass man. Fascism and Nazism took the condition of the masses as a decadence to be purified: Fascism through the elimination of corruption and dissent; Nazism through the elimination, as well, of its ethnic minorities. Communism took the conditions of the masses as an injustice to be corrected: through the elimination of private ownership and dissent, and the erection of an elaborate bureaucracy. [Thanks to Communism's anti-Fascism and romanticization of the proletariat, it has been forgotten that Fascism and Nazism were primarily working-class movements joined by the intellectuals and bourgeoisie; and that Communism was a movement of intellectuals joined by the peasantry in societies without a large working class.] All three took the spiritual flame of revolution and anti-colonialism and, in a recapitulation of the history of every major religion, codified it so that it had an answer for everything, institutionalized it so that power was concentrated in an elite, and maintained that power through continual mass sacrifice (sacrifice of one's own material wealth, sacrifice of one's own people in the struggle against the outside enemies, sacrifice of the impure within).

Every poet in the 20th century believed (believes) in the literary version of the spiritual flame of revolution: the transformative power of the word. (And how could they not, given the nature of poetry itself?) Nearly every poet in the 20th century has, at one time or another, ardently believed in one of these new world religions. (And those who did not, believed in a state of continual revolution without institutions, or, not too dissimilar, in poetry as its own religion.)

Since the rise of mass man, poets have, with few exceptions, viewed the condition of the masses as that of degeneracy (the Fascist and Nazi critique), though few have actively admitted the Fascist and Nazi solutions. In the 19th century the poets' response was individual retreat: either into the vanishing countryside or into the anonymity of the passers-by in the city. In the 20th century they have believed in the power of themselves, an elite, to transform the masses—usually through a trickle-down theory of popular culture. They have formed ephemeral exclusionary institutions (movements) and spoken in religious phrases ("purification of the language of the tribe," "rectification of names") and military terms, like "avant-garde," which, as Baudelaire said, assumed both militancy and military discipline.

Microcosms of the new religions, these movements launched

attacks, codified their opinions, petrified through excommunication into unyielding little monoliths. Author as authority, reader as follower: conspirators together, both believing that if only the others heard this message—or even the message of poetry itself—the world would change. ("People are dying every day for the lack of it.")

Who can read the exuberant manifestoes of modernism—burn the libraries, flood the museums, no more classics—without feeling sick, now, at the end of a century that has done, over and over, precisely what Marinetti and Ball and Tzara thought would be so swell? [Breton's "The simplest Surrealist act consists of dashing down into the street, pistol in hand, and firing blindly, as fast as you can pull the trigger, into the crowd" has already become quaint.] Who cannot help but wonder: after an actual 20th-century-style revolution of the word, what would happen to the old words: purged, tortured into compliance, reeducated?

Are there more than a few poets in the 20th century whom one can admire as citizens? Were there, in the babble of prophets, any that were true? [Today I happened to read *The Little Review* questionnaire of 1929. To the question "What do you most look forward to in the future?" Mina Loy replies: "The release of atomic energy."]

In the name of progress and in the name of tradition, a heap of bones, many of them the bones of poets. How can poets still invoke these values? Poetry lives simultaneously inside its historical moment and outside the historical continuum. To deny either, to mistake one for the other, has always been disastrous.

In the name of the group, a heap of bones. Poetry is written in spite of, or at the fringes of, the movements [the great Surrealist poets are not French], the political parties, the churches, the arts bureaucracies, the universities, the state. Collective strength is dependent on the elimination of subversion, and the poem is always sub-version, the underground version, the version that comes from some painted cave in the head.

The only belief that is salutary for poetry is the belief in poetry, which is never simple, and even less simple to maintain. Now, at the century's end, with the end of the ideologies and the imminent break-up of certain nations, the disease and threat of the next century will be nationalism, ethnocentricity, and all forms of excluding the other. Under the pressure of the expanding population, anyone not *us* will be seen as the cause of our misery. In poetry, if only for a moment, we are all us, all others—an us of others, and all of us talking.

[1988]

Sōgi's Renga to Himself

The end: so soon: cherry blossoms:

Cherry blossoms: sudden breeze: nightfall collects in the fluttering shadows: Through the shadows: there: over the rooftops: the mountain dimly aglow in moon and haze: In moon and haze this path I walk: is the path of thought: This path of thought: where the dream came: where the dream went back: She went back: she who came but could not be seen: over the endless hills of grass: Endless grass: brittle with frost: the path uncertain: Uncertain path: told only by that which is trampled: withered: grass:

Withered grass: why: do bugs creak their love for autumn: when autumn rushes their end: Rushing to the end in roaring wind: typhoon: terror and rage: Rage erases the sky: cloudless: transparent: the moon: Moon: the gate at Kiyomi Barrier opens: dawn floats over the river: Sumida River: when: would I ever be here again: to wake again on this shore: To sleep again on this shore: I cannot share this with her: she left me here: Here: my thoughts were spoken once: on a hill with no name: on a hill of flowers: Flower hill: I've given up the world: but who: can resist this transient spring: Spring: the mist that screens the world guides me home: Mist will guide me home: to wait for the smoke to drift from my pyre: In the drifting smoke of their miserable fire: salt collectors wait for the moon to rise: They wait for the moon that lights their labor: the autumn moon they hate: The autumn moon I hate: his promises that vanished: dew dripping off the grass as night falls: Nightfall: which: house is my husband going to:

Which house is he going to: he'd cross any woman's field: fields cover everything: Fields cover every place he crosses: at home they wait: and wonder if he'll come back: Wondering if I'll come back: why: I came aboard this boat: set for the point where waves meet the clouds: Where waves meet the clouds: in a sea of weeping: desolate: bitter sea: Bitter sea: China is here: beneath this same sky: beneath this same misery: The sameness of misery: even in Japan: anyone alive suffers: Alive and suffering: cherry blossoms blossom by the hut: spring rushes to its end: Spring rushes to its end: at the edge of the hills: the village in a screen of mist: Through a screen of mist: the wake of the moon coming down: birdsong breaks through with the morning light: Morning light: dewdrops fizzle: why: wake just to say goodbye: We woke to say goodbye: his coat had covered us: now cold wind is my quilt: Wind for a quilt: long day turns to night: still no word: No word: even desire withers: the heart that would never forget forgets: Forget: better forget: than a habit of miserable neglect.

In miserable neglect: yet: the decent life: even in a ruined house: overgrown with weeds: Even in a ruined house overgrown with weeds: flowers blossom for those who know what flowers mean: Flowers: in their moment: bright dresses: robe of mist: In the robes of mist: the path through the fields is lost: The path lost: another day of temple bells: nothing was learned: Nothing learned: though I know the Laws I cannot find the Way: Can't find the Way: 80 years: old as the Buddha: and no clarity: No clarity: the moon grows bigger: it does not light my mind: My mind: in the east: mist rising: the weight of desire: The weight of desire: in autumn the wind will come into the pines: he will come if you wait: I wait: some other: draws him to the cedar at her gate: My gate creaks: but the path to it: open as my pain: As open as his pain: seen through the fields: gathering wood for the temple: He gathers wood: frost falling on his sleeves: frost on frost on frost on the moss:

Frost on the moss: can't sleep: the weight of my troubles through the winter's night: Winter night: the moon even colder: dimming with dawn: Dawn: out in the reeds: a crane parades its sorrow with every cry: Every cry: the waves of desire: the wild

wind and waves: Wild waves: will: this government: ever bring
peace to the mountains and rivers: Mountains and rivers: will:
the land not fall to ruin: the peasants to ruin: Ruined peasants:
the harvest they awaited: frozen in autumn frost: Autumn frost:
grasses and grains: brown and withered around the hut: Around
the hut: the sound of washers beating wash: geese in the twilight
crying: Crying: the moon: uselessly moves on: I lie in this weight
of bitter troubles: Bitter trouble: he never came: I thought it was
the rain: but the rain's long gone: Gone: knowing what's missing
makes it worse: And worse: could: he have heard me say: I hope
he forgets: why: should he forget: He forgets: his letters stop:
the only words are carried by the wind:

Carried by the wind: blossoms already fallen: what: is left as
nightfall comes: Nightfall comes: spring comes: the old capital:
warm days its only pride: Only pride: a flutter of light: so real
and so unreal: the world: This world: haze for an anchor: the
boat drifts off: Drifting: this scene: moon rising: aglow on the
water: Aglow on the water: autumn night: uselessly moves on:
dawn breaks on the shore at Akashi: Akashi shore: a deer cries
longing: his mate somewhere far: Far off: he'll: kill himself on
the mountain of desire: Desire: why: brush away such dust:
when: such dust is everywhere: Dust everywhere: the stones on
the floor: all that's left of the palace: What's left of the palace:
grass and shrubs entangled: In the tangle: wind: picks out the
seedling rice: Rice: fireflies: they keep their troubles silent: This
silence: but my heart glows through the hidden love:

Hidden love: was it: her sleeve: or the morning haze: In the
haze: even spring still bitter: crossing the hills alone: Alone: this
wasted life: an old crane left behind: Left behind: I hope: to live
to see the autumn: but what: hope could autumn bring: What
hope of autumn: whole years move on through this long night:
Long night: even the moon moving on: that: it may not give me
pleasure: No pleasure: the sky drizzles on the drizzle on my face:
Face: rain: sky: gather in the misery of my heart. My heart: the
storm rushes in from the mountain above: Above: mountain

path through the gathering clouds: Clouds gather: falling rain for the waterfall that propels the Yoshino rapids: Yoshino rapids: do not: ask about the distant past: The past: how: did it vanish with no trace: No trail: my hut: moon shining on the tangling weeds:

Tangled weeds: the hills colored by colorless drizzle: Drizzle colorless as his cold drained heart: His heart: how: could I have let it: define my world: This world of desire: where all I desire: is a little bottle: to end this life of desire: To end: and be reborn: on the lotus throne: Lotus: raindrops: a summer shower: linger on the petals: then fall: Falling: as: wind breaks the clouds: I wake: from this: unfinished dream: A dream: I woke and saw a faint shadow: cast: myself: my old age: in this: dying light.

[1499/1991]

Two
WORLD BEAT

THE PRESENT

[*January–June 1989*]

Outside his window a man stood in a phone booth all day, pretending to make a call. Inside his window he sat in a room on the fourth floor, typing.

Wars were continuing in thirty-one countries, wars that had already killed over 7,500,000 people. Fourteen of the wars had lasted more than a decade; one was more than thirty years old.

A friend, whom he hadn't heard from in the last year, phoned. They caught up on old friends. One had died from AIDS. Another had died from AIDS. One had written the screenplay for the most successful movie of the year, and was now more unbearable than before. Another had become famous overnight: in the last six months she had given 700 interviews in a dozen countries. Another was still making false teeth and was the same. One, previously unathletic, had suddenly taken up skiing and was working at a ski resort. Another had won a large literary prize, which he deserved. A couple they had known in London had moved to New York and divorced. The ex-wife, a hunchback, had somehow had her hump removed, and was now making costumes for a transvestite theater company. The ex-husband had been found murdered, and the case was unsolved. As for his friend, nothing much was new.

The plants producing the radioactive material for nuclear weapons were leaking, and had been leaking for years. False reports had been issued to obscure these facts.

For a while it was thought that the plants would have to be closed and the production of nuclear weapons halted. This was clearly impossible, and yet the cost of repairing the plants would be enormous. It was therefore decided to change the safety regulations, so that the plants could operate safely again.

Along the highways, there was a craze for Fantasy Motels. The room with a waterbed set into an undulating floor of sand-colored carpet, like a blanket on a beach, with murals of surfers, the piped-in sound of waves crashing, and breakfast served in a beer cooler. The arctic igloo, a dome of white plastic blocks in bluish light, with a polar bear skin rug for a bed. The Lovers' Lane with artificial trees and painted vistas of city lights seen from a hilltop, and the bed an actual '57 convertible Chevrolet.

A gondola bed in the Venice Suite; in the King Tut Room, a sarcophagus bed; in the Prehistoric Cave a slab of rock under a fresco of galloping bison. A tent in an oasis for an Arabian Night; a log cabin hunting lodge for those who dreamt of trapping; a lunar landscape where one slept in a replica of the Gemini space capsule. For the literary, the Moby-Dick Room, where the bed was a dinghy and one entered the bathroom through gaping jaws. And yes, the Happy Days Café Suite in the Royale Hotel in West Bend, Wisconsin, where the bed was a giant sandwich and the whirlpool bath a cup of coffee.

Faith Popcorn, the president of Brain Reserve, a company specializing in these motels, explained their appeal: "There's a lot of fear and boredom out there. People want to experience adventure, but without any risk."

The new President, as far as one could tell, had the personality of a drunk at a party. His speech was idiosyncratic to the point of incommunicability, full of idioms of his own invention, like a man in love with his own voice and jokes. He liked to shake hands with a small buzzer hidden in his palm. On his first day in office, he delighted or bored his visitors and staff with a calculator that squirted water. Like a drunk, he had been, in the campaign, at one moment effusively sentimental, at the next nasty.

In the three months between the election and the inauguration, the new President emulated Teddy Roosevelt. He devoted himself to sport. Baseballs, footballs, and even horseshoes were thrown, and members of the small finned and feathered species were slain by bullet and hook. All of his major appointees were excellent at tennis.

Outside of Agra, home of the Taj Mahal, in the village of Badh, Titu Singh was a happy child until he turned three. Then he became melancholic, and would fly into a rage when anyone called him Titu. He would say, "My name is not Titu. I am Suresh Verma. I have a radio shop in Agra. My wife's name is Uma, and we have two sons." He would point to his parents and say, "These are not my parents. I'm just passing through here. My real parents are in Agra." Titu claimed that he, Suresh, had been murdered one night as he was returning home from work. Two gunmen had attacked him, and a bullet had gone through his head.

Titu's uncle went to Agra and found the Suresh Radio Shop on Mall Road. It had been owned by one Suresh Verma, who had been murdered five years before, exactly as Titu had described it. Suresh had left a widow, Uma, and two sons.

Uma and her parents drove out to the village to meet the boy. As they got out of the car, Titu hugged her parents, and then looked angrily at Uma: "Whose car is this? What happened to my Fiat?" Uma had indeed sold the car.

They took Titu back to Agra, where, as Titu, he had never been. He directed them to the shop, walked in, and immediately asked who had built the new showcase. It was a new showcase.

The autopsy report on Suresh Verma showed that the bullet had entered through his right temple, ricocheted off the skull, and exited under the right ear. Titu's right temple had a curious dent, and beneath his right ear was a starburst birthmark.

Uma was photographed with the boy. She said: "I know it is Suresh. But I realize no purpose can be served. Our relationship will never be the same."

As the skin of the airplane ripped, the stranger sitting next to her was, in a second, sucked into the night and the Pacific below.

The baby's feet tied to the slats, the crib covered with cobwebs.

In Uganda, the minimum monthly wage was 490 shillings. The price of a bunch of bananas was 500 to 800 shillings.

In the town of Mbarara, the Makeru Shalalukash Baazi—Christ in His Second Incarnation—was venerated. She was a four-year-old girl.

In the town of Mbuya, burning crosses had been seen in the sky. The Virgin had appeared, promising to create a stream whose water would cure AIDS.

The followers of the Holy Spirit Movement of Alice Lakwena, a young fish vendor, would walk into battle silently, standing erect, their bodies covered with an oil that could ricochet bullets back to the enemy rifles. They threw stones which transformed, in mid-air, into hand grenades. In this manner, many thousands in the Movement had died.

At the Museum of Modern Art he examined an enormous glass display case containing four or five petrified and moldy sausages and, nearly indistinguishable from them, a petrified and moldy piece of dog shit.

The new Vice President, having served in both, was asked what the difference was between the House of Representatives and the Senate. He replied: "In the House you can get a bunch of guys and go down to the gym and play basketball. You can't do that in the Senate." He was asked why he wanted to be Vice President. He replied: "It seems like a good career move."

Things for sale: Elvis Presley's first driver's license, dated 1952 ($7,400). Elvis Presley's card from the Memphis Public Library, dated 1962 ($650). Elvis Presley's electrocardiogram tape, from the day he died, August 16, 1977 ($8,000).

He walked into the police station and told them he could no longer live with his guilty conscience: Ten years ago he had murdered an old woman in the course of a robbery.

The woman was a passer-by on a street he'd forgotten. The police searched their files and came up with an unsolved case from around that time. Charged, he protested his innocence: the details were entirely different. Yes, he was a murderer, but not that murderer. He was standing trial for the wrong crime.

Americans believed they were living in the decade of the country's greatest prosperity. In middle-class families, however, for the first time since the Depression, it became necessary for both parents to work.

In 1,200 suburban towns, infants and small children were left during working hours at identical roadside buildings called Kinder-Care Centers. These were operated like fast-food franchises, with the materials and programs produced by a central office, and a quickly trained staff which was paid the legally allowable minimum wage.

Parents of infants, when they returned in the evening, were given a report, written in the first person, on the baby's sleeping, eating, diaper changes, and development that day. One report began: "Mommy, I have been trying to say mommy but it did not come out yet but when it does, you will be the first to know."

The new President took important members of the Congress on a tour through the private living quarters of the White House. He showed them the Monet and Cézanne paintings hanging in the sitting room, and the needlepoint rug his wife had taken ten years to complete. In the bedroom, they admired the photograph of the President's mother hanging over the bed, the radio tuned to a country music station, and the wallpaper of exotic birds that did not repeat a single bird. He took them into the bathroom, where everyone examined the cosmetics and was amused to see that the Presidential couple threw their wet towels on the floor. Then, back in the bedroom, the President photographed each Congressman and his wife sitting on the bed.

Fluorocarbons from refrigerators and aerosol spray cans were rapidly depleting the ozone layer in the upper atmosphere, which protects the earth from ultraviolet rays. Enormous "holes" were reported over the North and South Poles, and the situation was alarming for most of the earth. Major cities, however, were far safer, as they were protected by their own pollution.

She described her childhood: "I grew up in a multimillion dollar beach house. My mother had semitrailers full of garments, lots of jewelry, lots of precious metals. You can't imagine how strange my life has been. My mother always taught me that I was the reincarnation of John F. Kennedy. I'd sit in restaurants and think: 'Those people have no idea who's sitting over here.' When I started hearing about all of JFK's affairs and so on, I'd think: 'Boy, I have some bad karma to work out.' When people would criticize Caroline, I would say, 'That's my daughter you're talking about.' I was always convinced that one day I'd be assassinated again."

On a train he sat across the aisle from a famous novelist whom he recognized. The novelist chatted with his wife, made frequent notes in a small notebook, and read the stories of Chekhov. He, however, read a magazine devoted to gossip about movie stars and fell asleep. He dreamed he was reading a book written in the most crystalline prose, but when he awoke at his station he had forgotten every word.

The new Vice President gave the people of Hawaii a lesson in geography: "Hawaii has always been a very pivotal role in the Pacific. It is *in* the Pacific. It is a part of the United States that is an island that is right here."

He received a catalog of 348 self-help books for small children. These included the "Help Me Be Good" series: 29 books, each accompanied by a "read-along" audiocassette, so that a child could study the illustrations without adult assistance. The titles were: *Being Lazy, Being Forgetful, Being Careless, Being Messy, Being Wasteful, Overdoing It, Showing Off, Being a Bad Sport,*

Being Selfish, Being Greedy, Breaking Promises, Disobeying, Interrupting, Whining, Complaining, Throwing Tantrums, Teasing, Tattling, Gossiping, Being Rude, Snooping, Lying, Cheating, Stealing, Being Bullied, Being Bossy, Being Destructive, Fighting, and *Being Mean.* According to the catalog, 36 million of these books had already been sold.

The mass murderer was scheduled to be executed in a small town in Florida. Hundreds of people had gathered for the event, hoping there would not be another stay of execution. The local McDonald's hamburger franchise had advertised: "Free Fries If He Fries."

A friend told him the plot of a novel he was writing: During the Second World War, Hitler had, as a safety precaution, created a double who was groomed to look, move, and speak exactly like him, in order to appear in his place at public events. Forty years later, this double is living in a retirement village in Arizona, when he discovers that Israeli agents, mistaking him for the real Hitler, are on his trail. On the lam, he happens to meet up with an elderly Englishman who had once been Field Marshall Montgomery's double. The bond of doublehood transcending politics, Monty's double helps Hitler's double to escape. Safe at last in some remote part of the world—this part had yet to be worked out—Hitler's double turns out not to be a double at all. Hitler had sent the double into the ill-fated bunker, and had escaped by assuming the double's real identity. Hitler, of course, must now kill Monty's double, the only person on earth to know his true identity.

The average American car ran 18 miles on a gallon of gas. In Sweden they were manufacturing cars that ran 70: in France they had developed one that ran 100. It would have been cheaper to give every American, for free, a new car that went only 40 miles on a gallon of gas than to extract all the oil needed to supply the existing cars.

In prison for murder, after years in prison for rape, robbery, and burglary, he escaped, and held two small children hostage until the police shot him dead. What was unusual was that he was completely blind.

The Lieutenant General, now Assistant Secretary of Defense for Drug Policy, defended the practice of randomly testing government and military personnel for drugs: "Random testing is an honor. I like to be random-tested. It tells me I'm clean."

At the 42nd Street subway stop, passengers entering and leaving the train were forced to step over a man lying completely naked on the platform.

Heinrich Heine, in Paris in 1832, had written: "Near the Porte St. Martin was a deathly pale man on the damp pavement, struggling for breath: staring bystanders said that he was dying of hunger. My companion reassured me, however, that this same man died every day on another pavement in a different street—in fact, that this was his way of earning a living: the Carlists were paying him for this performance in order to arouse the people against the government. It would seem, however, that the pay for this work is pretty poor, since many of these people actually do die of hunger."

"Dear Doctor: I am currently involved in a wonderful relationship with my sister. I'm 24, she's 20. For many years we tried to deny our mutual attraction. However, in the last year we have come to realize that societal restrictions are less important than a true meeting of souls. What started as gentle strokes and fondling has escalated into the most caring sexual relationship I have ever experienced. Last month she mentioned how nice it would be if we could have a child. Last night, as we were snuggling, she brought up the idea again. I felt that although it's a nice idea, the risk of genetic disease outweighs the benefits. On the other hand, I'm no medical expert. My question is: What are the odds of having a healthy child?"

When someone died, it was the custom for friends and relatives to visit the funeral parlor, sign their names in a register, and look at the face of the deceased, embalmed and laid out in an open coffin. This was, however, a time-consuming procedure, particularly as one had to change beforehand into properly somber clothes. The Gatling Funeral Home in Chicago solved the problem by instituting 24-hour drive-in viewing. Without leaving one's car, one could sign the book and see the deceased on a closed-circuit television screen. Nursing homes hired buses to drive their patients through, when one of their own had died, without the bother of loading and unloading so many elderly people so many times. Mr. Gatling claimed that the system was particularly useful when the deceased left both a wife and a mistress: the mistress could drive through while the wife remained inside. Some viewers had been known to stare at the television screen for an hour.

Keeping pace with inflation, the supermarkets in that country were raising their prices every four hours.

The new President spoke: "We need to keep America what a child once called 'the nearest thing to heaven.' And lots of sunshine, places to swim, and peanut-butter sandwiches." With his granddaughter on his knee, he declared that the revitalization of the education system would be the top priority of his administration. When asked if he planned to restore any of the money for education cut from the budget by his predecessor, the answer was no. The new President declared that he would wage war against drug addiction. When asked if he would allocate new funds for this war, the answer was no. When asked how he planned to wage this war, he replied: through education.

Things for sale: A hand grenade ($19.95). A booby trap: "can be screwed directly into an explosive charge for instantaneous detonation or coupled to a detonator cord for remote firing" ($14.95). A ballistic knife, the "knife that shoots": "can be fired up to an effective range of 30 feet," with penetration "three times that of a manual stab" ($79.95). A trigger activator, which enables a semiautomatic rifle to fire 1,200 rounds a minute ($19.95). A laser sight, for point-and-shoot assassination capability up to 500 meters ($495). "Sexy Girls and Sexy Guns—The Video": "14 outrageous Southern California beauties firing some of the sexist machine guns ever produced. Girls in string bikinis and high heels blasting UZIs, MAC-10s, M-16s, MP-5s, AK-47s, M-14s and more." ($49.95).

Things to read: *Semi-Automatic Rifles:* "A top-notch book for those who find military-style self-loading rifles interesting for their history, intriguing for their engineering design, and a pleasure to shoot. Only a few other nations allow their citizens the privilege of handling these fascinating arms. In America, we the people grant ourselves the right to own them—a fact that makes this nation unique for its greatness."

Places to go: The North China International Shooting Academy, outside of Beijing. Under the auspices of the State Council's Ministry of Machine Industry, tourists may fire a variety of rifles, submachine guns, anti-aircraft guns, and anti-tank rocket launchers.

In the Bhati villages of Rajasthan, no one could remember a local wedding, for weddings take place at the bride's house and there were no Bhati women. The Bhatis, it is said, were too proud to suffer the impoverishment of paying dowries. Brides were found in neighboring communities, but were expected to follow Bhati custom: at the birth of a female child, the mother must immediately place a bag of sand on the infant's head, suffocating her. Now, with changing times, among the 10,000 Bhatis, there were 50 girls, all under ten. One of the eldest, the only girl in a school of 175 children, was locally considered to be the incarnation of a goddess: How else could she have survived?

It was the custom to give condemned criminals the meal of their choice on the night before they were executed.

Charlie Brooks requested T-bone steak, French fries and cat-sup, Worcestershire sauce, rolls, peach cobbler, and iced tea.

Ronald O'Bryan requested T-bone steak (medium-well to well-done), French fries and catsup, whole kernel corn, sweet peas, lettuce and tomato salad with egg and French dressing, iced tea with sweetener, saltines, ice cream, Boston cream pie, and rolls.

Jesse de la Rosa requested Spanish rice, refried beans, flour tortillas, T-bone steak, tea, chocolate cake, jalapeño peppers.

Jeffrey Barney requested two boxes of Frosted Flakes and one pint of milk.

Chester Wicker requested lettuce and tomatoes.

John Thompson requested freshly squeezed orange juice.

Charles Rumbugh requested one flour tortilla and a glass of water.

Stephen Morin requested unleavened bread.

Thomas Barefoot requested chef's soup with crackers, chili with beans, steamed rice, seasoned pinto beans, corn "O'Brien," seasoned mustard greens, hot spiced beets, and iced tea.

Michael Evans, Joseph Starvaggi, Raymond Landry, Leon King, James Paster, and Carlos Deluna requested no food at all.

On either side the bank is lined with trees, but there is no river. The river is sand. Rain comes, the flood rushes the branches, bones, and trash miles downstream. In a few hours the river again is sand.

Young women of marriageable age stand before the young men of marriageable age, who whip them.

Their staple is sorghum: grown, gathered, ground by the women. Meat, hunted by the men, is also eaten. Girls are encouraged to have their teeth removed as a sign of beauty, making it difficult for them to eat meat, leaving less for the men to share.

They practice ritual scarification, female circumcision. They tell the future by throwing sandals in the dirt. It is assumed that most of them are now dead in the civil wars and ensuing famine.

Late at night, the dim, hysterical voice on the telephone of the friend in the other country, alive and left to wonder what other friends were left alive.

The story went that, as each line of students fell to the bullets, a new line rose to take its place, singing—they still sang it—the Internationale. That line was in turn erased, and in turn replaced.

The story went that this heap of unsinging dead was doused in gasoline and set aflame exactly as the First Emperor had burned the books. It was no consolation that the books had survived because they had been memorized by so many.

The next morning he woke, and suddenly remembered a movie he had seen in his childhood, a low-budget 1950s science-fiction film. Two bearded professors are standing before a strange machine with flashing lights. It is a time machine, and the inventor is demonstrating its use to his colleague.

He sets the dial for five thousand and something, and places a soda bottle in the machine. It disappears, and moments later a weird Cubist bottle from the future takes its place. He puts in a fountain pen, and receives some strange writing implement.

The colleague, impressed, wonders whether the Phi Beta Kappa Society, of which he is naturally a member, exists in the future. He puts his "key," inscribed with the three Greek letters, into the machine. A misshapen medallion appears with some words scratched on it.

"Why, it looks like Greek! You studied classics, Professor, what does it say?"

"Yes, it *is* ancient Greek . . . And it says . . . 'Help us!'"

[1989]

THE MONTH OF RUSHDIES

March 15, 1989. After the thousand and one magical realist novels, with their daffodils falling from the sky and ancient crones giving birth to pig-faced children—novels desperate to recapture from the movies some small piece of the art of narrative by creating imagery that cannot be adequately represented on the screen—the genre has finally produced its masterpiece. Yet, as might be expected, it is not a novel at all, not even a book, but a tale that exists only in bits and pieces in the newspapers and on radio and TV, in oral transmission and cocktail party chatter. It is a plot that is still unfolding, and strangely, or not so strangely, it is the story of a magical realist novel: *Once upon a time there was a man who wrote a book which a billion people didn't like. They tried to kill him for it, and ended up killing each other. Few of these people had even seen the book, yet all, friend and foe alike, found that it revealed their own worst natures . . .*

I speak of course of the sprawling metafiction that is being engendered by that sprawling metafiction called *The Satanic Verses*. Today, the Ides of March—though the date, given the intellectual constriction of the protagonist, is surely arbitrary—is the deadline set by the Ayatollah Ruhollah Khomeini for the execution of Salman Rushdie. (And an execution, unlike sudden or slow death, creates its own, suspended yet fixed time: an endless pause until fate is enacted, executed.) So rather than yet another expedition to the moral high ground—that territory already thick with rhetoric—it may be a day simply to unravel the tangled plot, to try to get the story straight, as we wait for the next night of this fantastic tale:

Salman Rushdie was born to an upper-class Muslim family in Bombay in 1947, the year of Indian independence. At thirteen he was sent to England for a gentleman's education: Rugby and

83

Cambridge. His family, meanwhile, moved to Pakistan, where Rushdie joined them after graduation. His brief stay in Karachi a disaster, he was soon back in London, where he became a British citizen and worked for ten years as an advertising copywriter while attempting to write fiction. A fantasy novel, *Grimus,* written for a science-fiction prize, was published in 1974 and quickly forgotten. In 1981, however, his second book, *Midnight's Children,* became an international success. A magical realist novel about the children born at the moment of Indian independence and their descent from exhilaration to despair, it was the first novel to emerge from the contemporary urban chaos (in this case, of Bombay) rather than the "timeless" India of the villages. More important, after generations of Indian writers whose language was more English than the English, Rushdie's book was written in the accelerated, jazzy speech of the city streets. He was, incredibly, the first Indian to write extensively in Indian English, and he had the enviable position of being a Joycean with an entirely untapped language at his disposal.

Midnight's Children provoked endless debate in India for its savage portrait of Mrs. Gandhi—who threatened to sue Rushdie for libel—and her martial-law Emergency of 1975. India allowed copies to be imported, but there was no Indian edition for many years. In 1983 he published *Shame,* which was, in many ways, a shorter version of the previous novel, this time set in Pakistan. Once again, his portrait of a ruler, the Pakistani dictator General Muhammad al-Huq Zia, set off a storm, and the book was banned in that country.

Rushdie became a celebrity in England, usually paired in opposition with England's other novelist-of-Indian-origin-in-residence, V. S. Naipaul. Where Naipaul stood for Queen and Thatcher, and made a career out of ridiculing Third World countries, Rushdie criticized England's ethnocentrism and institutionalized brutality against its minorities. Naipaul, in his tweed suits, lived as a squire in a country cottage; Rushdie, in a loose kurta, was part of the trendy left-wing literary set in the city.

The topic of his next novel was almost predictable: the masses of Asian immigrants in London. Rushdie had always been the first in his territory, and here was an opportunity for which he was perfectly suited. After two centuries of Orientalism and the thousands of novels and accounts of Englishmen abroad, the time was overripe for a story of the reverse migration and peregrinations: an epic of Occidentalism.

With an advance of $850,000 from Viking/Penguin, he clearly set out to write the Anglo-Indian *Ulysses*. What he wrote was *The Satanic Verses:* a dense and very funny novel, filled with characters who mirror each other and ten years' worth of news stories and objective correlatives from England, India, Pakistan, and the U.S., much of which will float by most readers outside of those countries: the baby stoned to death on the steps of a mosque in Lahore; the film star Dimple Kapadia (here called Pimple); the woman bandit Phoolan Devi; the man in California who swindled money from widows by claiming he had to buy back his soul from the devil; the New York restaurant Takesushi; the Tamil star M. G. Ramachandran, who played various gods in the movies and then became governor of his state and a little god himself; the massacre of children in Assam; the housing scandals in London; and so on. Like nearly everything of interest coming from England these days—so reminiscent of American narratives in the 1960s—the book is largely set in the apocalypse of Thatcher London, with its race riots, police violence, cars burning in the streets. It is a novel whose language is relentlessly brilliant on every page, and yet the pages never quite add up to a novel, for they paper over some enormous holes.

Following Dickens, the novel has scores of memorable minor characters, and one can imagine a wonderful version of *The Satanic Verses* composed entirely of these passers-by: a panorama of the city. Instead, hundreds of pages are devoted to its two protagonists who, forced to stand for nearly everything, sink under the weight of their allegorical trappings. One, Gibreel, is a Bombay film star who turns into an evil angel and ends up as a tragically jealous lover, reenacting *Othello;* the other, Chamcha, is an Indian who has become the perfect Englishman, a benevolent Satan who turns into a goat—regaining his human form only when he vents his long-suppressed rage at the Raj—and

who, in the cloying and transparently autobiographical end of
the novel, returns to Bombay for a reconciliation with his dying
father and Mother India.

Within this story, Rushdie has incorporated another novel. [In
a 1984 interview with the Australian magazine *Scripsi*, Rushdie
described two novels he was then working on. They have clearly
been joined together in *The Satanic Verses*. It is one of the com-
monest mistakes of modernism: to assume that the two disparate
works one happens to be writing can form a counterpoint to one
another in a single piece.] This second novel extends the explo-
rations of religious fanaticism begun in *Shame* into yet another
virgin territory: the secular—not to mention satirical—use of the
Quran. And it is this second work that not only partially under-
mines the novel, but ruined the author's life.

Islam is the fastest-growing religion in the world (as it is in the
United States, particularly among blacks) not only because it has
replaced Communism as the sworn and effective enemy of the
colonialist West, but also because it offers the last refuge against
the social and psychological commotion of the century: modernism, doubt, criticism, feminism. Of the three monotheisms, Islam
is, for many reasons, the purest, the least affected by change, and
the least subject to variation over the centuries. First, its founder
lived in historical time, and Muhammad—a merchant, general,
politician, and prophet of Mecca—considered himself merely an
ordinary man whom God had selected to receive His message.
There is, in orthodox Islam, no folklore about his life: no miracles or displays of supernatural power, no local variants taking
on lives of their own beyond the Quran. Second, it is the only
major religion whose founder also personally created a theo-
cratic state (and killed people to create that state); thus a model
for Islamic society was spelled out in detail from the beginning.
Third, its book—which legitimized Islam for the other peoples
of the book, the Jews and the Christians—is the only one of the
three that is actually written by God (and then dictated by the
archangel Gabriel directly to Muhammad). As such, it is the first
and last word, and it is inviolate: it cannot be translated, and it is

the only Arabic text where the vowels are written out, to avoid mistakes in its recitation. Furthermore, Islam takes very seriously the Jewish commandment against graven images: the text is all. It is the only major religion without a sacred figurative iconography, and even purely secular representational art is rare, for it is blasphemous to rival God as Creator. In the 9th century *Hadith* literature, for example, owning representational paintings is considered as disgusting as keeping a dog inside one's house: the reason why Arab and Persian artistic impulses were mainly channeled into the calligraphic and architectural arts.

Islam begins and ends with the Quran. It has not only not had a Reformation: it has not had the artistic adaptations or elaborations of the other religions—the thousands of versions of Jesus or the Buddha or the Virgin Mary. [What it has had are centuries of theological and legalistic debate over passages in the Quran. It is important to remember, thinking about the power of the Ayatollah Khomeini, that the Shiites, unlike the Sunnis, believe that a new cycle began after the death of Muhammad, and that the secret meanings of the Quran are continued to be revealed to the Imams.]

Rushdie has leapt into this iconic vacuum with two chapters in which his character Gibreel (Gabriel) dreams of the founding of Islam. It is a comic burlesque version, reminiscent of the scene in Buñuel's *Viridiana* where the beggars reenact the Last Supper: Muhammad is called Mahound (a medieval English derogatory name for the Prophet); Mecca is Jahilia (Arabic for "darkness"); a scribe named Salman—more than a post-modern joke: Salman was a Persian companion of Muhammad, and is particularly beloved by Iranian Shiites—deliberately changes the words dictated by the angel Gabriel to Mahound; and countless aspects of Quranic law are turned upside down. Worse, in a story within the story, the whores in the Jahilia brothel take on the names and identities of Mahound/Muhammad's wives and reenact events occuring in the outside world.

The irony, given the ensuing events, is that the novel would have been much stronger without these two chapters (and two further chapters, where a young woman prophet, clothed in

butterflies, leads a village of Mecca pilgrims into the sea), which
have little to do with the rest of the book. But Rushdie clearly
felt—despite his later disavowals—that an all-out parodic assault
on the basic tenets of Islam was long overdue. The novel is full of
self-reflexive lines, like: "Looks like he's trying deliberately to set
up a final confrontation with religious sectarians, knowing he
can't win, that he'll be broken to bits." Or: "Your blasphemy,
Salman, can't be forgiven. Did you think I wouldn't work it out?
To set your words against the Word of God." With one hand, he
ties himself to the stake: "A poet's work is to name the unname-
able, to point at frauds, to take sides, start arguments, shape the
world and stop it from going to sleep. And if rivers of blood flow
from the cuts his verses inflict, then they will nourish him." With
the other hand, he slips the knots: "Fortunately, however, I am
only telling a sort of modern fairy-tale, so that's all right; nobody
need get upset, or take anything I say too seriously. No drastic
action need be taken, either."

But, as the *coup de grâce*, he titled his novel after the one flaw in
the Quranic carpet, the "Satanic Verses" themselves. According
to a contemporary legend, Muhammad, having met considerable resistance to his attempt to eliminate all the local gods of
Mecca in favor of the One God, recited some verses which admitted three popular goddesses as symbolic Daughters of Allah.
Later Muhammad claimed that the verses were dictated to him
by Satan in the voice of Gabriel. Thus the Quran, as Mircea
Eliade has pointed out, is the only divinely revealed text which
was subject to revision—which of course becomes another post-
modern joke.

The Satanic Verses was published in England on September 28
of last year with predictable results: the book was a critical and
commercial success. A few days later, Viking/Penguin received a
letter from a dentist, Dr. Hesham el-Essawi, chairman of the
moderate Islamic Society for the Promotion of Religious Tolerance. Dr. Hesham wrote: "I would like to invite you to take
some kind of corrective stand before the monster that you
have so heedlessly created grows, as it will do worldwide, into

something uncontrollable." The publishers ignored the letter.

Controversy was expected in India and Pakistan, where Rushdie had had problems with his previous novels. Asked by an Indian newspaper on September 18 whether he had heard rumors that the book would be prohibited, Rushdie replied: "That's news to me . . . But it would be absurd to think that a book can cause riots. That's a strange sort of view of the world." Rajiv Gandhi, however, was facing important state elections in a country with 100 million Muslims, and where ethnic and sectarian strife had escalated under his wobbly regime. Under pressure from fundamentalists in Parliament—"No civilized society should permit it"—Gandhi directed the Finance Ministry to ban the book in India. Rushdie replied with scorn in an open letter: "Mr. Prime Minister, I can't bring myself to address finance ministries about literature." Dom Moraes and nineteen other writers and editors sent a letter of protest, and were themselves later threatened.

In England, meanwhile, there was a blizzard of telexes, faxes, letters, and photocopied excerpts of the book sent by various Muslim groups to organizations, embassies, and governments around the world. The book was banned in Pakistan, Saudi Arabia, Egypt, Somalia, Bangladesh, Sudan, Malaysia, Indonesia, Qatar, and South Africa—though it was unlikely that more than a few copies would ever reach many of those countries. Pressure was put on Viking/Penguin to withdraw the book, and on the Thatcher government to ban it and prosecute Rushdie under the still-existing blasphemy laws (which, almost needless to say, only applied to Christianity) or the Race Relations Act or the Public Order Act—or to extradite Rushdie to an Islamic country.

Rushdie, scheduled to address an anti-apartheid and anti-censorship rally in South Africa—the title of his speech, paraphrasing Heine, was "Wherever They Burn Books, They Also Burn People"—was asked not to come after Muslims threatened a "holy war" against everyone involved with Rushdie's appearance.

On November 21, the Al-Azhar institute in Cairo, seat of Islamic theology, ruled that the 46-nation Islamic Conference Organization should take action against "this distortion of history."

British Muslims, frustrated in their attempts to stop the book, held mass rallies through December and January in towns in the north of England with large Muslim populations, including Oldham, Bolton, and Bradford (home of the Brontë sisters). Local Labour Party MP's, supported by the Bishop of Bradford, attended the demonstrations, where copies of *The Satanic Verses* were burnt. On January 28th, 8,000 people gathered in protest in Hyde Park in London.

The demonstrations set off flurries of indignant letters and articles, and impassioned defenses of the freedom of the word from Rushdie. This was, no doubt, the kind of controversy Rushdie had anticipated, and probably desired. What no one could have foreseen, however, was the mayhem that broke out around the world with the publication of the book in the United States, five months after the British edition. [The book appeared in the stores in the first week of February; its official publication date was February 22.] The story is so full of subplots, daily developments and reversals that it is best—at this early stage, while it is still unfolding—told through a day-to-day chronology:

February 12. Police open fire on anti-Rushdie demonstrators storming the American cultural center in Islamabad, Pakistan. Five are killed and 100 wounded. Later in the day, the American Express office is sacked.

[Given the fact that the book, already banned in Pakistan, is written by a British citizen and has been available for months in England, the attack on American offices seems peculiar. In the following days it becomes evident that Rushdie is merely a pretext, and that the demonstration has been orchestrated by the defeated opposition party, the Islamic Democratic Alliance, in league with various fundmentalist groups, as a way of destabilizing the recently elected government of Benazir Bhutto, who at the time was out of the country on a state visit to Beijing. Bhutto, a Harvard graduate who spent years in exile in London, is seen by fundamentalists as far too Westernized. Worse, she is a woman who has announced that she will lift the Quranic restrictions on women instituted by her predecessor, General Zia. The demonstrators chant slogans referring to Bhutto with "vulgar epithets for female animals."

The leader of the demonstrations turns out to be Kausar Niazi, who had once been a minister in the government of Benazir Bhutto's father, Zulfikar Ali Bhutto, who was overthrown and executed by General Zia. In the Bhutto days, Niazi's nickname was "Whiskey"—an ironic echo of the movie mogul in *The Satanic Verses*, "Whiskey" Sisodia—due to his well-known fondness for alcohol and dancing girls. His sudden defense of orthodox Islam surprises even the fundamentalists.]

February 13. Police kill three and wound sixty in demonstrations in Srinagar, India, the capital of the predominantly Muslim state of Jammu and Kashmir. The city completely shuts down for three days. [Again, Rushdie is a pretext for a display of Kashmiri nationalism, including those who wish to secede from India, or merge with Pakistan, or overthrow the Rajiv Gandhi government.]

The American Embassy in Islamabad issues a statement: "The U.S. government in no way supports or associates itself with any activity that is in any way offensive or insulting to Islam or any other religion." [There is no mention of the fact that the First Amendment to the U.S. Constitution guarantees freedom of speech—"any" speech.]

In London, Rushdie responds: "The thing that is most disturbing is that they are talking about a book that doesn't exist. The book that is worth killing people for and burning flags for is not the book I wrote . . . The common characteristic of the people who are fulminating against this book is that they haven't read it." [As Rushdie well knows, had they read it they would have been no less angry.]

February 14. In Iran—five months after the publication of the book, and three months after it was first reviewed in the Iranian press—Radio Teheran announces the *fatwa* (decree) of the Ayatollah Khomeini: "The author of the book entitled *The Satanic*

Verses . . . as well as those publishers who were aware of its contents, have been sentenced to death. I call on all zealous Muslims to execute them quickly, wherever they find them . . . Whoever is killed on this path will be regarded as a martyr." Khomeini warns other governments against attempting to interfere with his commands.

The British Foreign Office asks for a clarification.

[Khomeini's death warrant occurs at a particularly delicate moment in Iranian history. The long and finally inconclusive Iran-Iraq war has left hundreds of thousands of dead and the country devastated. Khomeini's own health, at age 86, is failing, setting up a struggle for succession. Both the West and the Soviet bloc are eager to win the lucrative contracts for reconstruction. Within Iran, a faction led by Speaker of the House Hashemi Rafsanjani—the so-called "moderates," although they have been responsible for the execution of thousands of political opponents—is urging closer ties with the West. Those around Khomeini still favor complete isolation from the secular world. Khomeini is, above all, a brilliant tactician: by calling for Rushdie's death, he will provoke such opposition from the West so as to effectively subvert Rafsanjani's conciliatory gestures.]

In Pakistan, "Whiskey" Niazi claims that emissaries are already on their way to London to assassinate Rushdie. "My prediction is that he will be eliminated in the coming few months." He also calls for the death of any Pakistani attempting to protect Rushdie.

Rushdie: "It is not true this book is a blasphemy against Islam. I doubt very much Khomeini or anyone else in Iran has read the book . . . Frankly, I wish I had written a more critical book."

February 15. A "National Day of Mourning" in Iran. Many thousands demonstrate outside the British Embassy. All Viking/Penguin books are banned. The "moderate" Rafsanjani reveals that, in a meticulously planned campaign, Rushdie was hired by British Intelligence—working with the CIA, Italian intelligence, and Zionist publishers around the world—to write a book that would discredit Islam. An Iranian charitable organization—set up to care for the relatives of demonstrators killed in anti-American protests in 1963, and now proprietor of a large supermarket chain—offers a reward of $3 million to any Iranian or $1 million to any foreigner who kills Rushdie.

Rushdie goes into hiding with his wife, the American novelist Marianne Wiggins, protected by armed guards supplied by Scotland Yard.

A promotional tour of eleven U.S. cities is canceled. The French publishing house of Christian Bourgois announces it has dropped its plan to release the book, after threats to the publisher's family and staff. In New York, television and radio programs have difficulty finding well-known writers or publishers willing to publicly support Rushdie. They are, quite simply, fearful for their lives. Only one internationally known writer, the Egyptian Nobel laureate, Naguib Mahfouz, condemns the Iranian action as "intellectual terrorism." Given his position as the best-known Muslim writer (still living in a Muslim country) in the world, it is an act of considerable courage.

The Netherlands—the first country to officially respond—cancels a forthcoming visit of their Foreign Minister to Iran.

There is still no comment from the British government. Harold Pinter and a group of writers and publishers deliver a letter of protest to 10 Downing Street. [Although it is unprecedented for a national leader to publicly call for the execution of a foreign citizen living in his own country, Mrs. Thatcher—called Mrs. Torture in *The Satanic Verses*—is, naturally, slow to come to the aid of one of her harshest critics. Had it been, say, Kingsley Amis, the gunboats would already be steaming up the Persian Gulf. It should also be remembered that Thatcher has instituted the strictest censorship laws, by far, of any Western democracy, and that she herself, like Khomeini, unsuccessfully attempted to prohibit the foreign publication of a book she had banned in England—Peter Wright's bland memoir of his British Intelligence days, *Spycatcher*—even taking the Australian publishers to court in that country.]

The Iranian Embassy to the Vatican asks the Pope to join the crusade against the book. A senior Vatican official replies: "It's their problem, not ours. We have enough of our own, especially with all the books and films which cast doubts on Jesus Christ Himself."

February 16. The Iranians raise the bounty by another $3 million. A mullah in Peshawar offers 500,000 rupees—only $30,000, it's a poor country—to any Pakistani who "kills the infidel." Muslims in Sierra Leone proclaim their solidarity in the fight against "the new plot by world oppression against Islam."

An Italian newspaper asks the Iranian Ambassador to the Holy See, "If Mr. Rushdie were in this room, unarmed, and you were armed with a pistol, would you pull the trigger without any hesitation?" He replies: "Yes, certainly I would. The law of God is clear."

Britain announces that it will temporarily freeze its recent efforts to improve diplomatic relations with Iran. Pakistan recalls its foreign ambassadors to discuss the situation.

114 French writers issue a statement of solidarity with Rushdie. In the U.S., however, various writers' and publishers' organizations, but few individuals, condemn the death threat. The largest book chain, Waldenbooks, citing the safety of its employees and customers—although as yet there have been no threats—orders the book removed from its 1,200 stores across the country. Employees are instructed not to talk to the media. Harry Hoffman, president of Waldenbooks and a former FBI agent, declares that the defense of freedom of speech is a problem for government, not for business (even if the business is dependent on freedom of speech): "Waldenbooks is not Congress . . . Our people are not Foreign Service officers, members of the diplomatic corps, or soldiers sworn to protect the rights of citizens . . ."

[The immediate capitulation to Khomeini by publishers and booksellers is indicative of the terror that Islam now strikes in the West, particularly since the de-demonization of Communism. Imagine if the threat had come from a nation of equally minor international power: say, if Castro had demanded the banning abroad of books by Heberto Padilla. The reaction would have been a smile or a shrug. The Cubans, of course, do not commit acts of terrorism in the United States, but, as no one seems to notice, neither do the Iranians or any Islamic group: with a few minor exceptions, all attacks on Americans have occurred abroad. In the U.S. there have been far more attacks *on* Iranians and Arabs, particularly Palestinians, than by them. On the other hand, it is also true that, in the Media Age, where there is wide-spread panic and hype concerning acts of violence that might, but have not yet, occurred, those acts will inevitably occur, in-spired by the publicity.]

February 17. The President of Iran, Ali Khameini, suggests that if Rushdie apologizes, "this wretched man might yet be spared."

The British government announces it will retain its staff in Teheran: "The publication of books in this country has abso-lutely nothing to do with the British Government."

Canada bans imports of the book under a law prohibiting "hate literature." [Enacted a few years ago under pressure from Jewish groups, this law was meant primarily to ban neo-Nazi writing. In Canada, an advanced democracy, there are people who have been jailed for publishing books that claim that the Holocaust was a hoax.] A large book chain there, Coles Book Stores, announces they will not sell the book.

Most Western European governments denounce Iran, recall-ing minor officials or canceling state visits. Publishers in West Germany, Greece, Turkey, and Japan drop plans for the book, but those in Finland, Norway, and Italy decide to go ahead with their editions.

In the U.S., the second and third largest chains, B. Dalton and Barnes & Noble, pull the book off their shelves. [With the book-chain ban, the controversy becomes a local issue. American wri-ters realize that the timidity of the chains will doubtless have future repercussions: The three chains account for 30% of all book sales, and if ideologues can force a book out of the stores, publishers will be reluctant to bring out books that might give offense. The writers finally begin to speak out publicly as indi-viduals. The U.S. government, after years of saber-rattling on the question of terrorism, still has not commented on this rare instance of an actual national threat.]

The book, not sold at the chains and long sold out from the independent stores, is completely unavailable in the U.S., and will remain so for the next three weeks while Viking/Penguin reprints its edition. Thus *The Satanic Verses* continues to be a book very few, through the hottest days of the controversy, have even seen.

February 18. Responding to yesterday's hint from the President of Iran, Rushdie issues a tepid three-sentence apology: "As the author of *The Satanic Verses,* I recognize that Muslims in many parts of the world are genuinely distressed by the publication of my novel. I profoundly regret the distress that publication has occasioned to sincere followers of Islam. Living as we do in a world of many faiths, this experience has served to remind us that we must all be conscious of the sensibilities of others."

Less conscious of the sensibilities of others, the novelist Anthony Burgess writes: "We want no hands cut off here. For that matter we want no ritual slaughter of livestock, though we have to put up with it . . . If they do not like the secular society, they must fly to the arms of the Ayatollah . . ."

American writers and literary organizations line up to condemn Iran and the book chains, and to demand that President Bush—who is generally becoming known as the White House Hamlet—make up his mind to respond.

[American comment is largely marked by hyperbole and false analogy. The Holocaust, for both sides, is a popular motif. Susan Sontag writes: "We feel superior to those Germans who in 1933 and 1934 didn't protest when their Jewish colleagues were being fired or dragged off in the middle of the night to camps. It's clear that the threat of violence by people perceived as fanatics is very terrifying . . . But we have to be brave." (Nearly all the "celebrity" writers remark on their own bravery in finally speaking out, as though Iranian tanks were patrolling Soho.) The anti-Rushdites, revealing that they don't watch television, wonder how Jews would feel if the Nazis were made a subject for comedy.

Exiled writers take the occasion to recall the imprisonment, censorship, and threats they received in their own countries— not one of them noticing that Rushdie is the first outlaw of the global village: the man for whom exile is not possible. (Even with the death of Khomeini, he will remain the Enemy of Islam; even with the passage of years there will be someone, somewhere, who won't forget. As Rushdie had written in 1984, "The modern world lacks not only hiding places, but certainties.")

There is a similar tendency, among the American writers, to reduce Rushdie to themselves: authors of works that go out into a world populated exclusively by like-minded souls. A remark of extraordinary chauvinism by Ralph Ellison will be repeated often, and always favorably, throughout the affair: "A death sentence is a rather harsh review."

Writers who normally are on the barricades condemning American imperialism call for military action against Iran. Rightists claim that celebrities like Rushdie are news, but not the faceless writers imprisoned and murdered by Communist regimes. Leftists claim that celebrities like Rushdie are news, but not the faceless masses imprisoned and murdered by right-wing regimes. Nearly everyone prefaces their remarks with sympathy for the wounded sensibilities of the Muslims, but nearly no one wonders why it is only religious ideologues whose sensibilities can be wounded—the rest of us have far stronger constitutions, and are never distressed by the social demands of the divinely motivated.]

February 19. The Ayatollah responds to Rushdie's apology: "Even if Salman Rushdie repents and becomes the most pious man of time, it is incumbent on every Muslim to employ everything he's got, his life and wealth, to send him to hell."

The British government responds that they view the Ayatollah's comments with "great concern."

The British Museum puts the book on its locked "restricted" shelves, normally reserved for pornography. On the front page of the *News of the World* Rupert Murdoch warns Muslims in England to behave. On the front page of the *Star,* Murdoch offers one-way tickets home for any Muslim "fanatics." A sports newspaper offers a million pounds for Khomeini's head.

In New York, Cardinal O'Connor denounces the book, which he has "no intention" of reading. [Although murder is theoretically contrary to the Judeo-Christian and other extant sacred traditions, and religious leaders are generally no longer given to ordering executions, not a single major religious organization or individual in the world has come to Rushdie's defense.]

February 20. The 12 European Economic Community nations agree to recall their ambassadors from Teheran. The British announce they are withdrawing their entire staff. The U.S. government has no comment.

The book is banned in Papua New Guinea, Kenya, Sri Lanka, Tanzania, Sierra Leone, and Thailand. In Japan, the English-language edition is banned. In the Comoros Islands, all foreign magazines are banned—they might contain extracts. In Zanzibar and Malaysia possession of the book is punishable by three years in prison. In Venezuela—a country with almost no Muslims—even reading the book will draw 15 months imprisonment.

In the *Washington Times*, an influential newspaper despite the fact that it is owned by Sun Moon's Unification Church, columnist Patrick Buchanan attacks Rushdie for his support of Daniel Ortega and the Sandinista government: "Since he is so high on Danny the Red and so down on Mrs. Thatcher, maybe Sal will want to fly down to Nicaragua and seek sanctuary there."

February 21. Iran, in turn, withdraws its ambassadors from the EEC nations. Canada, Sweden, Australia, Norway, and Brazil recall their ambassadors. West Germany cancels an important trade agreement. Britain asks Iran to remove its chargé d'affaires from London. The Secretary General of the United Nations appeals for Rushdie's life. The Archbishop of Canterbury calls for the blasphemy laws to be strengthened and extended to include other religions. Canada lifts its ban against the book.

President Bush, at last, makes an informal statement, in response to a reporter's question: "However offensive that book may be, inciting murder and offering rewards for its perpetration are deeply offensive to the norms of civilized behavior." He has no comment on the removal of the book from American bookstores. When asked whether he supports economic sanctions against Iran, he replies that he doesn't know. [He is not asked why murder and writing differ only in their degrees of offensiveness.]

In the U.S., amidst the paper storm of statements by writers and literary organizations against Iran and the book chains, seventeen prominent Catholic writers publish a letter attacking Cardinal O'Connor.

February 22. The Ayatollah reaffirms his position, and further remarks: "As long as I am alive I will never allow liberals to come to power again, nor shall I allow any deviation from our policy . . . and I will continue cutting off the hands of all Soviet and American mercenaries."

The President of Iran—the "moderate" who had implored the novelist to apologize—touring Eastern Europe, states: "An arrow has been shot and is traveling toward the heart of the blasphemous bastard Rushdie."

In the first comment from the Arab world, Sunni religious leaders meeting in Mecca declare that they will put Rushdie on trial in absentia for heresy, and possibly sue Rushdie in British courts for slander. They emphasize their legalistic approach to the controversy. No Arab political leaders have commented on the case.

The Archbishop of Lyon attacks the book and declares his "solidarity with all those who endure this pain in the spirit of dignity and prayer." This provokes President Mitterand's first public response, attacking "dogma" and "fanaticism" as "absolute evil."

The Japanese government issues an understatement: "Encouraging murder is not something to be praised."

It is the official publication date for the book in the U.S., and the newspapers are full of advertisements declaring solidarity with Rushdie. In New York, 300 writers march in freezing rain outside the Iranian Mission to the United Nations; with the exception of former Yippie Abbie Hoffmann, there are no recognizable book-jacket faces in the crowd. A few hours later, 3,000 people line up to attend a mass reading (indoors) by famous authors sponsored by PEN. The hall can only seat 500, and 400 of the places are already occupied by the press. Those who manage to get inside are frisked, and hear selections from the book— chosen by a Viking editor—and mainly forgettable statements read by Susan Sontag, Joan Didion, Mary Gordon, Robert Stone, the actress Claire Bloom (who qualifies as the wife of a writer, Phillip Roth), Diana Trilling, Don DeLillo, E. L. Doctorow, and others, some of whom are accompanied by their publicists. [One wit points out that any one of these writers has, in years of lunching with editors, prevented the publication of more books than the Ayatollah could manage in a hundred lifetimes.]

Christopher Hitchens reiterates the Holocaust motif by declaring that we must all "don the yellow star." Gay Talese recites the Lord's Prayer. Larry McMurty tells how he was once threatened by a six-foot-six transvestite in his bookstore. The anthropologist Lionel Tiger recalls his bar mitzvah. Frances Fitzgerald states, with more liberal sympathy than historical foundation, that "to see the Ayatollah as the representative of Islam is like seeing the Grand Inquisitor as the representative of Christianity"—which is precisely what, for millions, the Grand Inquisitor was. Norman Mailer speculates at length on the scene of the hit man attempting to collect his bounty, and then uses the occasion to attack Tom Wolfe, who is sitting in the audience.

Robert Massie, president of the Authors' Guild, calls for a boycott of the chains. A drop in sales being more terrifying than a bomb in the mall, B. Dalton and Barnes & Noble later announce that they will resume selling the book, when it becomes available again.

In the day's most intelligent comments, Edward Said, while defending plurality and free speech, articulates these "questions from the Islamic world" (although he himself is a Palestinian Christian): "Why must a Muslim, who could be defending and sympathetically interpreting us, now present us so roughly, so expertly, and so disrespectfully to an audience already primed to excoriate our traditions, reality, history, religion, language, and origins? Why, in other words, must a member of our culture join the legions of Orientalists in Orientalizing Islam so radically and unfairly?" [To carry Said a step farther, it could be argued that Rushdie has, in a sense, become his enemy, V. S. Naipaul. Rushdie is, after all, the best known writer of Muslim background in the West, and yet he has now become an "insider," writing exclusively for the West, who in fact reinforces, through parodic excessiveness, the West's distaste for things and events in the Third World.]

February 23. The Holy War Organization for the Liberation of Palestine, a pro-Iranian group holding three American hostages, vows vengeance against Rushdie.

French and West German publishers, under pressure from writers and newspapers in their countries, announce that they will publish translations of the book after all.

The Israeli publisher says that it is rushing the Hebrew translation, despite opposition from both Jewish and Muslim groups. The leader of the Orthodox Degel Hatorah Party attacks the book: "Muhammad is portrayed as going to a prostitute. Imagine if someone had written that about Moses."

In London, a nearly forgotten folksinger from the 1970s, Cat Stevens, surfaces as a Muslim convert named Yusuf Islam, and declares that Rushdie should die. "If he turned up on my doorstep asking for help, I'd try to phone the Ayatollah Khomeini and tell him exactly where this man is." Radio stations around the world immediately ban his records, which provokes heated debate in the Top-40 world on censorship and the question of whether an artist can be separated from his political views. Stevens/Islam himself, however, is delighted: since his conversion he has disowned his old records and attempted to remove them from the market.

February 24. In Bombay, police open fire on anti-Rushdie demonstrators as they approach the British consulate, killing twelve and wounding forty in a three-hour battle. 1,300 are arrested.

In the loftiest assessment to date, Carlos Fuentes in the *Los Angeles Times* declares that Rushdie is an avatar of the Imagination, of a Bakhtinian dialogue set against the monologue of organized religion, the state, the multinational corporation. The Rushdie case becomes a kind of morality play, where the novel, which only offers questions, is locked in combat with the sacred text, which pretends to have all the answers.

February 25. The British government asks the Soviet Union to mediate on the Rushdie crisis in their forthcoming talks with Iran. Both the Soviet government and Soviet writers have so far been silent on the question. The Soviet Ambassador to Britain states, with no apparent irony, that the situation "clearly shows the need for respect for religious feelings and traditions as well as tolerance for the politics and values of others."

5,000 Muslims march against Rushdie in The Hague; 1,000 in Oslo; 2,000 in Copenhagen.

February 26. A bomb at the British consulate in Karachi, Pakistan, kills a Pakistani guard.

The Ayatollah meets with the Soviet Foreign Minister Eduard Shevardnadze, and announces that he wants closer ties between the two nations to counter the "devilish acts of the West." This is the first visit to Iran by an important Soviet official since the 1979 revolution. Khomeini also suggests that the solution to Gorbachev's problems may be found in conversion to Islam: "I want to open for Mr. Gorbachev a window to a great world—that is the world after death, which is the eternal one."

In New York, ten to fifteen thousand Muslims demonstrate in front of the offices of Viking/Penguin, chanting—in an unintentional advertisement for Rushdie—"Shame!" It receives almost no news coverage. A thousand march against the book in Paris. Many thousands demonstrate in the holy city of Qom.

February 27. Jean-Marie Le Pen, leader of the National Front in France states: "What Khomeini has just done with revolting cynicism is exactly what I fear for France and Europe, and this is the invasion of Europe by Muslim immigration."

Georges Sabbagh, director of the Near East Studies Center at UCLA is asked by *Time* magazine if Muslims have a right to kill Rushdie. He replies: "Why not?"

In Mali, the book is banned and the President directs the ministers of defense, information, territorial administration, basic development, and agriculture to make sure that it is enforced.

The Prime Minister of New Zealand, David Lange, refusing to sever trade relations with Iran, states that he sees no reason why New Zealand sheep herders should suffer because of "a threat made to a bookwriter in London."

In Germany, *Der Speigel* quotes Rushdie from an earlier interview: "If Woody Allen were a Muslim, he would not live very long."

February 28. Iran gives Britain one week to repudiate Rushdie, or it will cut off all political relations. The Soviets offer to mediate, and mysteriously hint that they may be able to effect a solution.

In Berkeley, California, two bookstores are firebombed: a branch of Waldenbooks and the well-known Cody's Books. It is the first actual violence in the U.S., though other bookstores and Viking/Penguin now receive daily telephone threats, and it is said that some Viking/Penguin executives are wearing bulletproof vests to work. President Bush announces that he "will not tolerate" such violence, but offers no specific protection.

The British novelist Roald Dahl denounces Rushdie as a "dangerous opportunist" who found a "cheap way" of getting "an indifferent book to the top of the bestseller list."

Sheik Ahmad Kaftaru, religious leader of Syria, declares: "The novel is worthy neither of reading nor respect, due to its lack of scientific, accurate or objective methods of research."

March 1. Advertisements by the International Committee for the Defense of Salman Rushdie and His Publishers, signed by nearly every well-known writer in the world, begin appearing in newspapers around the world.

Jacques Chirac, Mayor of Paris, states: "I am not confusing Muslims with fanatics, but . . . foreigners, once they are on our soil, must respect our laws."

March 2. Britain's Foreign Secretary, Geoffrey Howe, reacts to the Iranian ultimatum: "We do understand that the book itself has been found deeply offensive by people of the Muslim faith. We can understand why it has been criticized. It is a book that is offensive in many other ways as well." The Secretary also states that the book is "extremely rude" about Britain, and claims (falsely) that the book compares Thatcher's England with Hitler's Germany.

Rushdie, who has remained incommunicado, telephones an opposition member of Parliament to express his anxiety that Britain may be ceding to Iranian demands.

French companies announce they will slow down their purchase of Iranian oil. The group SOS-Racisme stages a demonstration against fundamentalism in Paris. The U.S. attacks the Soviet Union for "cozying up" to the Iranians. Thousands march against Rushdie in Dakka, Bangladesh, and stone the British Council Library.

March 3. Iran utterly rejects Britain's conciliatory gestures. Although there is no official announcement, it is widely rumored that Khomeini has set a deadline of March 15 for the execution to be carried out.

In the London *Times,* Lord Shawcross attacks the book for having been written without "any intention of contribution to scholarship."

In Khartoum, a huge demonstration. Thousands march in Kuala Terengganu in northern Malaysia.

March 4. At the British Embassy in Tokyo, demonstrators chant for Rushdie's death. Thousands riot at the airport in Karachi, looting the VIP lounge. In Hong Kong, petitions are circulated to ban the book. Demonstrations in the Philippines. An Egyptian mullah living in Teheran condemns Naguib Mahfouz to death for supporting Rushdie.

In England, a Conservative MP suggests transferring Rushdie to a missile-testing site in the Outer Hebrides to save the expense of protecting him.

On BBC television, an interviewer asks an Iranian diplomat: "Do you understand that we don't regard it as civilized to kill people for their opinions?"

March 5. Ahmed Jabril, leader of the Popular Front for the Liberation of Palestine—the group probably responsible for blowing up the Pan Am jet over Scotland last December—vows to kill Rushdie.

The Turkish Prime Minister, Turgat Özal, states: "A crazy man threw a stone in the well, and a thousand intellectuals are doing battle to get it out." No one knows if the crazy man is Rushdie or Khomeini.

Former President Jimmy Carter, not exactly known for his savoir-faire in dealing with Iranians, publishes an article titled "Rushdie's Book Is an Insult": "While Rushdie's First Amendment freedoms are important, we have tended to promote him and his book with little acknowledgment that it is a direct insult to those millions of Muslims whose sacred beliefs have been violated and are suffering in restrained silence the added embarrassment of the Ayatollah's irresponsibility." [Rushdie, in *Shame,* had written: "Autocratic regimes find it useful to espouse the rhetoric of faith because people respect that language . . ."]

March 6. The Vatican newspaper condemns the book as blasphemous: "It is certainly fair to ask what kind of art or liberty we are dealing with when, in their name, people's most profound dimension is attacked and their sensitivity as believers is offended." In various places in Italy, bookstores displaying the book have their windows smashed.

A bizarre development: in Ravenna, a group calling itself the Guardians of the Revolution threatens to blow up Dante's tomb unless the Mayor repudiates the characterization of Muhammad in the *Commedia*. The Mayor refuses—repudiate Dante!—and orders armed guards around the tomb.

In Jerusalem, the Chief Rabbi of the Ashkenazic Jews calls for a ban on the book in Israel: "One day this religion is attacked, and the next day it will be that one."

March 7. Iran breaks all diplomatic relations with Britain. In Iran, it is considered a victory for the anti-West, Khomeini faction.

March 8. Britain announces it will expel 20 to 30 Iranians living in England.

The Organization of Revolutionary Justice, a Lebanese group holding two American hostages, claims that—having "attentively read" the book and "studied the case"—it will attack the police protecting Rushdie "in order to reach him and execute him." A Syrian group, the Popular Front for the Liberation of Palestine, also announces that it will kill him. The Kuwaiti government attacks the book for its lack of "objectivity and scientific research."

Susan Sontag, testifying before a subcommittee of the Senate Foreign Relations Committee, asks why the U.S. government has not formally condemned Iran. She also points out that Federal law enforcement officials are supposed to protect the exercise of Constitutional rights—voting, registering in school, demonstrating, and so on—but have not been called out to defend the First Amendment right to publish, sell, and read books.

The FBI, rather than suggesting there are G-men undercover at the local Barnes & Noble keeping America safe for reading, decides to calm the public by claiming that there are now dozens of members of the Iranian Revolutionary Guard Corps in the U.S., posing as students. They also state that nearly half of the 800,000 Iranians currently in the country receive money from the Iranian government. They offer no evidence.

March 9. In Britain there have been no public events in support of Rushdie for three weeks. Various members of the House of Lords denounce Rushdie for ruining the possibly lucrative relations with Iran. The Chief Rabbi of the United Hebrew Congregation of the Commonwealth calls for legislation which will ban all inflammatory books. [Presumably he will personally be responsible for measuring the degree of flammability.]

A public reading of the book takes place in Berlin. Günter Grass resigns from the Akademie der Künste after they refuse to allow the reading to be held on their premises.

In Riyadh, Saudi Arabia, it is rumored that Rushdie is the owner of a London brothel where the women all have the names of the Prophet's wives.

In the U.S., *The Satanic Verses* appears in the stores again, and immediately becomes the best-selling book in the country.

March 11. On the Op-Ed page of the *New York Times,* Joyce Carol Oates complains about the pretension of "Insufficiently Famous Writers" attacking "Famous Writers" (including herself) for initial cowardice and later "self-promotion and self-righteousness."

March 12. In *The New York Times Book Review,* 28 writers from 21 countries send messages to Rushdie: "You must be firm and brave"; "Don't despair"; "Take good care of yourself"; and so on. Susan Sontag writes: "I hope you are getting some exercise and listening to music, dear Salman." In the strangest message, Joseph Brodsky claims that "the book itself asked for it," and then calls on writers to chip in for a bounty on the Ayatollah's head. [In an act of similar civility, British press magnate Robert Maxwell had already offered six million pounds to anyone who "civilizes" Khomeini.]

On another blasphemy front, Italian television, under pressure from the Vatican, bans a rock video in which the singer Madonna, wearing a black lace negligee, enters a Catholic church, passionately kisses a life-sized statue of a black saint, and receives the stigmata. Responding to the uproar with succinct

wit—qualities almost entirely absent in the Rushdie affair—
Madonna replies: "Art is controversial."

March 13. Three of the 18 members of the Swedish Royal Academy of Letters (which awards the Nobel Prize for Literature) resign when a committee statement, deploring censorship around the world, fails to include Rushdie.

March 15. The 46 Muslim nations, meeting in Riyadh, reject Khomeini's demand that they break relations with the West, and issue a statement condemning both Rushdie and Iran. The Egyptian Minister of the Interior states: "Khomeini is a dog. No, that is too good for him. He is a pig."

J. Danforth Quayle, currently serving as Vice President of the United States, declares that he has not read the book, but "obviously it is not only offensive but, I think most of us would say, in bad taste."

Despite the Ayatollah's deadline, Salman Rushdie manages to live through the day.

In 1984 he had written: "In the jungle of the cities, we live among our accumulations of things behind doors garlanded with locks and chains, and find it all too easy to fear the unforeseeable, all-destroying coming of the Ogre—Charles Manson, the Ayatollah Khomeini, the Blob from Outer Space."

[1989]

* * *

Postscript: Months and Months

Less than a month after withdrawing them, eleven of the EEC nations—all except Britain—returned their ambassadors to Teheran. No economic sanctions were ever imposed, by any country, throughout the controversy.

The United States government never made a formal statement or took an official position on either the foreign or domestic aspects of the case. The dozens of Iranian Revolutionary Guards who, according to the FBI, were posing as students in the U.S., apparently remained students.

No important religious organization or individual ever supported Rushdie.

Moscow's secret plan for ending the controversy was never revealed.

Although the Islamic world is generally perceived in the West as a monolith, no Arab leader or government, with the exception of Qaddafi in Libya, ever endorsed Khomeini, nor were there demonstrations in any of the Arabic-speaking countries. The Arabs—though many denounced Rushdie—universally declared that the *fatwa* was contrary to Islamic law at innumerable points.

In Brussels, two men—Abdullah al-Ahdal, head of the local mosque of the World Islamic League and considered the spiritual leader of Muslims in the Benelux countries, and Salem el-Beher, the mosque librarian—were both shot in the head inside the mosque. In an interview on Belgian television, Ahdal had criticized the death threat against Rushdie as contrary to Islamic law. A group linked to Iran, the Soldiers of Justice, claimed responsibility for the assassinations.

There was a half-day national strike in Bangladesh; fifty were injured in battles with police protecting British and American property.

Benazir Bhutto made her only statement on the book: "Because I am a Muslim, I have not read it."

Muslim writers in France signed a petition of support: "Against fanaticism and intolerance, we are all Salman Rushdie."

In Moscow, a group of writers founding the first Soviet branch of International PEN, condemned the death threat—the first comment by Soviet writers on the affair.

In Kaduna, Nigeria, demonstrators calling for the death of the novelist Wole Soyinka—who had written that Khomeini's "person, voice, thoughts, sayings, etc. etc." should be banned—rioted outside the British Consulate.

In Paris, a popular singer, Veronique Sanson, withdraw her song "Allah," after death threats. Cassettes naming various "enemies of Islam" were distributed among the local Muslim population.

On Charing Cross Road in London, the two largest bookstores were bombed for displaying *The Satanic Verses*. Bombs were frequent in bookstores around the country. A play on the Rushdie affair, *A Mullah's Night Out*, was renamed *Iranian Nights* after the cast became nervous. As late as May 27, 20,000 Muslims burned Rushdie in effigy in Parliament Square in London.

In an obscure controversy in Los Angeles, a low-budget film about Iranian exiles, *Veiled Threat*, scheduled for the annual American Film Institute Festival, was dropped, according to its producers, because of bomb threats. The Institute, however, charged that the filmmakers had fabricated the threats for publicity purposes.

In New York, the president of the Pakistan League of America politely requested that Rushdie be extradited and handed over for trial in an Islamic court. A group of Ayn Rand followers, the Committee for the Defense of the Free Mind, took out full-page advertisements in the newspapers condemning all anti-rational mysticism, the "religious right and the relativist left," and demanding U.S. military action against Iran.

Meanwhile, among the hundreds of thousands of students and workers demonstrating for democracy in Tiananmen Square in Beijing in May, 200 Chinese Muslims stood apart, holding signs which read "Death to Rushdie."

Most of the major European publishers—with the exception of Viking/Penguin, which was not invited—announced that they would be attending a book fair in Teheran in May, sponsored by the Iranian Ministry of Islamic Culture. Two American publishers, originally planning to attend, finally withdrew under pressure.

The Satanic Verses was translated into fifteen languages. In

France the book was published with a title page listing the support of the Ministry of Culture and twenty-one publishers. The translator's name was given as Alcofribas Nasier, the somewhat Moorish anagrammical pseudonym of François Rabelais. In Germany seventy publishers were listed; in Spain 18. In Brazil, no publisher would take on the book, and it was issued by the Ministry of Culture of the State of São Paulo.

The anti-Rushdie demonstrations were a boon to European neo-Fascist groups. In less than two months the German Republican Party grew by fifty percent. On the centennial of Hitler's birth in April, Turkish workers stayed home all day, out of fear. In France, Le Pen's National Front did extremely well in the municipal elections.

In a defeat of the so-called "moderate" faction in Iran, the Ayatollah Khomeini ousted his designated successor, the Ayatollah Hussein Ali Montazeri (who had refused to support the *fatwa*) as well as the Deputy Foreign Minister and the representative to the United Nations. In terms of domestic politics, the Rushdie affair was a remarkable victory for Khomeini: in the restlessness and discontent following the end of the Iran-Iraq war, he had rallied the nation and eliminated or converted many of his most powerful enemies. (Even Speaker of the House Rafsanjani was now calling on Palestinians to kill Americans "wherever they find them.") On June 3, Khomeini died. At his funeral hundreds of thousands of mourners tipped over his coffin to tear shreds from his shroud. With Khomeini's death, the *fatwa* would remain in effect forever, for only he could revoke it.

In July, Rushdie and his wife separated. Coming out of hiding, Marianne Wiggins revealed that they had moved once every three days since February.

A bomb intended for Rushdie blew up its owner in London on August 3.

A collection of articles on the case was commissioned in England by William Collins Son, a publishing house owned by Rupert Murdoch, and then canceled. A book on the case by the right-wing scholar Daniel Pipes was commissioned in the U.S. by Basic Books, a publishing house owned by Rupert Murdoch, and then canceled.

In September, Britain restored full diplomatic relations with Iran, after publicly acknowledging that the book had offended Muslims and that the government had taken no part in it.

The Satanic Verses remained for months at the top of the bestseller list, selling well over a million copies in English alone. Debate raged over whether to issue a paperback edition. In September 1989, Rushdie and Viking/Penguin made a secret agreement to publish the paperback in June 1990, if circumstances allowed. A poll of British booksellers a few weeks later revealed that more than half would not stock such an edition. In October, a confidential risk assessment for Viking/Penguin reported that the danger is "undiminished."

Rushdie had surely become the most famous writer in the world, author of the most famous novel of the 20th century. But, as in a fairy-tale pact with the devil, it was likely that he would never be able to enjoy his fortune. In hiding—in his unique form of house arrest—he wrote book reviews for British newspapers, thank-you notes to those who had supported him, and a fable for his son, *Haroun and the Sea of Stories*. For a year he made no statements, nor gave any interviews.

In early 1990, Rushdie launched a campaign of reconciliation, publishing essays and giving interviews to defend the book, clarify misperceptions, and state his position as a secular man who supported the rights of Muslim minorities in the West. On February 8, Khomeini's successor, the former President Ayatollah Ali Khameini, reaffirmed the *fatwa*. He called on all faithful Muslims to carry out the death sentence.

In April, Pakistan released a movie called *International Guerrillas* (spelled *International Gorillay* on its posters). In the film, a band of sinister international Zionists decides to destroy Islam once and for all by commissioning Salman Rushdie to write a book. Later—after many subplots, teenage girls swearing death to Rushdie with their dying breaths, and musical interludes—Rushdie is seen as a sort of Dr. No, a master criminal on his own island, surrounded by his private army. The bodies of international guerrillas of Islam are swinging from the palm trees. A new batch of prisoners is brought in. Rushdie picks up a scimitar and slashes their throats one by one. He holds the sword to his nose and takes a deep satisfying breath. Car chases, flying motorcycles, and heavy gunplay. A new band of heroes fights Rushdie's army. In the end they are defeated and brought before the evil novelist. Then, just as they are about to be dispatched, Qurans appear in the four corners of the screen shooting out electrical bolts that sizzle Rushdie to death. (The movie quickly became the biggest box-office hit in Pakistani history. Tapes of it were banned in Britain.)

In December, Rushdie's children's book was published. A few weeks later, on Christmas Eve, Dr. Hesham el-Essaway, president of the Islamic Society for the Promotion of Religious Tolerance in the United Kingdom, and the dentist who had first warned Viking/Penguin about the global ramifications of the book, released an astonishing statement from Rushdie:

> In the presence of his Excellency the Egyptian Secretary of State for Endowment and head of the Supreme Council of Scholars of Islamic Affairs, Dr. Mohammed Ali Mahgoub, and a group of Islamic scholars:
>
> 1. To witness that there is no God but Allah, and that Mohammed is his last prophet.
>
> 2. To declare that I do not agree with any statement in my novel *The Satanic Verses* uttered by any of the characters who insults the prophet Mohammed, or casts aspersions upon Islam, or upon the authenticity of the holy Quran, or who rejects the divinity of Allah.
>
> 3. I undertake not to publish the paperback edition of *The Satanic Verses* or to permit any further agreement for translations into other languages while any risk of further offense exists.
>
> 4. I will continue to work for a better understanding of Islam in the world, as I have always attempted to do in the past.

In a press conference, Rushdie said, "I feel a lot safer tonight than I did yesterday." In an essay, "Why I Have Embraced Islam," published a few days later in innumerable newspapers, Rushdie wrote, "I am certainly not a good Muslim. But I am able now to say that I am a Muslim; it is a source of happiness to say that I am now inside, and a part of, the community whose values have always been closest to my heart. In the past I described the furor over *The Satanic Verses* as a family quarrel. Well, I'm now inside the family . . . I believe that in the weeks and months to come, the language of enmity will be replaced by the language of love." (He did however stop short of withdrawing the book completely: It "is a novel that many of its readers have found to be of value. I cannot betray them.")

In the West, Rushdie's enemies took this as a desperate attempt to save his neck, while simultaneously promoting his new book. Most of his supporters attributed his statement to the exigencies of his life: solitary confinement had driven him crazy. There were the inevitable comparisons to Heberto Padilla's notorious recantation. Some thought he was joking, and some of his former allies revealed their anti-Muslim biases by viewing it as a betrayal. In fact, the conversion was foretold, like much of what subsequently happened, in *The Satanic Verses:* it was a small leap from the novel's deathbed reconciliation with his father to a reconciliation with the patriarchy of Islam.

"What I know of Islam," Rushdie wrote in his essay, "is that tolerance, compassion, and love are its very heart." In Iran, the newspaper of the ruling Islamic Republican Party reacted to the conversion: "If Rushdie's repentence and his return to Islam are seen as a sign of bravery, naturally it is necessary that he shows greater bravery and prepares himself for death. He will die anyway, but he will be better off to choose his way to eternal salvation courageously before a son of Islam fires the *coup de grâce.*"

Khameini, for his part, paraphrased Khomeini: "Even if he repents and becomes the most pious Muslim on earth, there will be no change in this divine decree."

When it was finally published, Daniel Pipes' book contained a remarkable piece of information: the name "Satanic verses" is an invention of 19th century British Orientalists. In Arabic (as well as the other languages spoken by Muslims) the verses are called *gharaniq*, "the birds," after the two excised lines about the Meccan goddesses: "These are the exalted birds / And their intercession is desired indeed." In Arabic (and similarly in the other languages) Rushdie's book was called *Al-Ayat ash-Shataniya*, with *shaytan* meaning Satan, and *ayat* meaning specifically the "verses of the Quran." As the phrase "Satanic verses" is completely unknown in the Muslim world, the title, then, implied the ultimate blasphemy: that the entire Quran was composed by Satan. The rest of the book was, in a way, almost irrelevant.

On July 3, 1991, the Italian translator of *The Satanic Verses*, Ettore Caprioli, was stabbed in his apartment in Milan. He survived the attack. Days later, on July 12, the Japanese translator, Hitoshi Igarashi, an Islamic scholar, was stabbed to death in his office at Tsukuba University in Tokyo. No one was arrested in either case.

The novel parallel to *The Satanic Verses*, then, the one that was still being written, had turned out to be a global epic that had unraveled from the old Italian pun of translation and betrayal. The "translated man" (as Rushdie called himself in *Shame*), translated from India and Pakistan to England, from Urdu to English, from Islam to atheism, is condemned to death for a mistranslation. He undergoes further translations: from society to solitary confinement, from speech to silence to speech, from atheism to Islam. His mistranslators are killed in the name of mistranslation, his translators wounded or killed for the crime of translation, and his novel itself a translation—thousands of translations—without an original.

In December 1991, a recantation of the recantation: Rushdie made a surprise appearance in New York, at a dinner honoring the First Amendment and freedom of speech at the Columbia School of Journalism. He stated that his conversion, the previous

December, was actually a failed attempt to "fight for the modern-
ization of Muslim thought" from within Islam, and that he had
never thought of himself as anything other than a "secular Muslim, who, like the secular Jew, affirm[s] his membership of the
culture while being separate from the theology." Claiming that
he had, at the time, "agreed to suspend—not cancel—a paperback edition," he now called for a "freely available and easily
affordable" edition.

With the recent release of the American prisoners in Lebanon,
Rushdie referred to himself as the "last hostage," and as a man in
a leaking hot-air balloon, sinking into an abyss. At Rushdie's
hotel room, the windows were covered with bulletproof padding,
the curtains drawn, the corridors filled with guards. He arrived
at the dinner in an armor-plated, bombproof limousine; at the
dinner itself, there were metal detectors, bomb-sniffing dogs,
and scores of plainclothes police, some of them with sniper rifles.
After the speech, no one was allowed to leave the room until
Rushdie was safely gone.

As the third anniversary of the *fatwa* approached on Valen-
tine's Day 1992, Rushdie revealed that he was marrying for the
third time. The identity of his bride was kept secret.

A consortium of publishers, human rights organizations, and
writers' groups announced their intention to publish an American paperback edition of *The Satanic Verses*, Viking-Penguin
having, with great relief, returned the rights to Rushdie. Two of
the largest publishers, Random House and Simon & Schuster, as
well as the Association of American Publishers, refused to join
the group.

The anniversary was marked by television appearances in England by Tom Stoppard, Günter Grass, and others; articles in
newspapers around the world by Nadine Gordimer, Paul
Theroux, Margaret Atwood, and William Styron; and a visit to
Washington by a delegation from PEN, asking that the lifting of
the *fatwa* be "a firm precondition of any renewal of diplomatic
relations with Iran." (There was no official response.) The Iranian newspaper *Jomhouri-Eslami* published reaffirmations of the

death penalty—not only for Rushdie, but also for his editors and publishers—from various political and religious leaders, under the headline, "A Divine Command to Stone the Devil." In England, the new literary editor of the *Guardian*, Richard Gott, argued, in the interests of world harmony, against a paperback edition: "I would prefer Salman Rushdie to retreat from the barricades, to abandon his role of politician, and simply to write, from the depths of some well-guarded obscurity—like Thomas Pynchon and J. D. Salinger." Rushdie, not amused, replied: "I refuse to be an unperson. I refuse to forego the right to publish my work."

[Here the narrative breaks off, and goes to press . . . with governments and publishers and the world at large returned to business as usual; with Rushdie, a spook condemned forever to nowhere, a chameleon on a mirror; and with his enemies, both the sincere and the manipulated, frozen on the verge of ending the story.]

[March 1992]

Travels in the Federated Cantons of Poetry

"Maybe what this country needs is a great poem."
—Herbert Hoover, 1932

In 1941 the literary magazine *Accent* published what was intended to be a complete bibliography of American poetry for the years 1930 through 1940. Only nonliterary poetry—inspirational lyrics and greeting card doggerel—was omitted. Read today, the list is astonishing: During those 11 years there were only 151 American poets, and they published 264 books of poetry. If one read only two books a month in that decade, one would have read every new book of American poetry.

This year's edition of the *Directory of American Poets*—itself an emblem of the age—includes 4,672 poets, all of them published, and all of them, incredibly, approved by a committee which determines that they are, in fact, poets. To read only one book by every living American poet—at the rate of one book a day, no holidays—would take 13 years, during which time another few thousand poets would have appeared.

And, in these Alps of truncated lines, at least a thousand poetry magazines appear on their own irregular schedules, like a thousand unsynchronized cuckoo clocks. It is a whole Switzerland of poets. Critics and anthologists may continue to pronounce on the state of the art, but no one has any idea what's going on, except in one's own valley and the immediately neighboring hostile or friendly valleys.

It was once a village where the neighbors chatted and feuded. Now American poetry is a little nation of citizens who are unknown to each other, a federation of cantons where the passes are snowed in and the wires down. In the last 25 years, these are some of the writers who have died with nearly all their work unpublished or out of print: H.D., Louis Zukofsky, Langston Hughes, Paul Blackburn, Charles Olson, Marianne Moore, Mina Loy, Frank O'Hara, Charles Reznikoff, Jack Spicer, Lorine Niedecker.

And at the other end, the disappearance of the younger poet, unable to get a message through:

In 1940, Oscar Williams' anthology, *New Poems*, had 36 American and British poets, two-thirds of whom were under 35, most of them under 30. Many of these young poets were already well known: Auden, Spender, Warren, Empson, Dylan Thomas, Schwartz, Rukeyser, among others.

In 1960, Donald Allen's *The New American Poetry* included 44 poets, again two-thirds of whom were under 35—with half of those under 30. Again, many of the young already had considerable reputations: Ashbery, Ginsberg, Snyder, O'Hara, Blackburn, Leroi Jones, McClure, Koch, to name a few.

In 1987 there were two anthologies of the "new": Andrei Codrescu's *Up Late: American Poetry Since 1970* had 103 poets, only 18 of whom were under 35, and none of them under 30. Of those 18, there were only a few whose names were even vaguely recognizable outside of their own circles. Douglas Messerli's *"Language" Poetries* included 20 poets, none under 30, 2 under 35.

As late as the late 1960s—mine is the last generation to remember this—if one had access to a good bookstore, it was possible to be aware of, to at least glance through, every new book of poetry. A new small press book or magazine was an event. In an issue of *Kulchur*, Gilbert Sorrentino reviewed a mimeo sheet of no particular interest only because it existed and such things were rare.

Switzerland: a proliferation of poets and their products not attributable merely to population growth or the rise of mass university education, let alone an epidemic of sensitivity. What has happened is that, in the literary ecosystem, the natural selection of poets has been thrown off-balance by the elimination of the poet's main predator, money.

To go back: In the late 1960s, disturbing phenomena: Beatnik bohemianism flowers into a national culture. Robert Duncan waves the banner: "The old excluded orders must be included: the female, the proletariat, the foreign; the animal and vegetative; the unconscious and the unknown; the criminal and failure."

Three movements:

1. Black nationalist poetry, with its own political agenda, with a huge and genuinely populist audience, effectively admits African-American speech into poetry (something the Harlem Renaissance, with the notable exception of Hughes, had refused to do), has a close and exciting working relationship with jazz and some rock musicians (the now-forgotten grandparents of rap and hip-hop), offers scathing commentaries on whites and white "verse," and brings in a great deal of African and African-American history, mythology, and religion previously absent in American poetry.

2. Poetry written and read against the Vietnam War, an extraordinary moment when American poets serve as citizens, witnesses, intellectual consciences of the nation (a role that poets routinely perform elsewhere on the planet). A democratic vision of a republic of letters and, as Clayton Eshleman later writes, one that seems to portend a "responsible avant-garde" for the post-Vietnam years.

3. Ethnopoetics—essentially an American revision and expansion of Surrealism, itself a response to a war and a prophecy of the next war—not only introduces a tremendous amount of American Indian and other indigenous works, but also presents a rereading of American literature, discovers all sorts of strange and forgotten poets, emphasizes oral performance and poetry rituals and talismans, translates a great deal of European modernist poets, offers new theories and practices of translation, and, perhaps most of all, proposes an image of the poet, based on the archaic, as a vital, necessary member of the community.

Blacks, Indians, foreigners, magic, hallucination as ultimate reality, the personal as political, public manifestations against the state—and the students, demanding that what they study be "relevant" to their lives. Poets, if not (with the exception of Ginsberg) national icons like rock stars, prominent among it all.

By 1970—things seemed to move quickly then—the traditional enemies of poetry, the universities and the state, had responded. Colleges began teaching contemporary poetry and offering courses and advanced degrees in something called "creative writing." [In 1914, the Dadaist poet and boxer Arthur Cravan, fulminating against the current vogue for art schools, had written: "I am astonished that some crook has not had the idea of opening a writing school."] Black studies programs were introduced (leaving the English Departments as they were: the domain of whites). Hundreds of universities and community arts centers supplemented their writing courses with regular series of poets reading their own works. Known for their political canniness and hatred for the arts, Lyndon Johnson founded and Richard Nixon ("They're all Jews") implemented the creation of the National Endowment for the Arts, while arts councils were formed in each state, all of them giving money not only directly to writers, small magazines and presses, but also to the mushrooming arts "service" organizations and their attendant bureaucrats, which were also handing out money and sponsoring readings, workshops, prizes, and fellowships.

Poetry, almost overnight, became a respectable middle-class career: "pobiz," as Nathaniel Tarn called it in the late 1970s. One could now graduate with a degree in Creative Writing, take a job teaching Creative Writing, and augment one's income with readings and grants. In the past, the exigencies of earning a living had discouraged all but the most committed (or more exactly, obsessed), and those who held on were nevertheless forced out into the world as workers, journalists, capitalists, bohemians—all of which, in turn, had nourished the poetry. Now anyone could remain forever on campus in the springtime of adolescent poetry-writing. And the artificially induced explosion of the pro-

duction of small presses and magazines would insure that everything written would find its publisher, if not its readers.

The poetry against the war ended long before the war ended.
Black nationalist poetry disappeared into Department corridors.
Ethnopoetics had no second generation. And the remnants of
the "avant-garde," enamored with continental theory, began
speaking in the wearying high-tech jargon of Comp. Lit. mono-
graphs, presenting their rabble-rousing manifestoes at the annual meeting of the Modern Language Association.

Switzerland: a sameness of lives producing a sameness of poetry. Today the typical mainstream American poem—taught in
the writing schools, winner of prizes and grants for its author,
published nationally—is anecdotal, descriptive, autobiographical, concerned exclusively with small matters, and invariably
written in prose syntax: *I open an old trunk in grandma's attic;
There was a dead elk I saw once in Alaska; We were ice-skating when
you told me of your parents' divorce.*

Switzerland: makers of cuckoo clocks. The poets call their
writing classes "workshops," and talk endlessly of "craft." In the
workshops a single gospel is taught: the function of poetry is to
discover the wonders of ordinary life, usually by means of far-
fetched simile. And the best students learn to twist their sen-
tences into traditional prosody, and employ an exotic *fin de siècle*
vocabulary.

A nation devoted to self-expression and the promotion of
one's self-expression. A land where everyone who plays the pi-
ano is a pianist. The poetry magazines publish photographs of
the poets larger than the poems themselves. Of the poets of the
pobiz generation, those now under 50, few seem to know much
about poetry itself, other than the work of those contemporaries
personally useful to know. (A degree in Creative Writing re-
quires no creative reading.) Few use their intelligence and skill to
write on anything else, to enrich the cultural or excoriate the
political. (In the disaster of Reagan America, were there five of
the five thousand poets who spoke publicly against it, except

when the NEA budget was cut?) Few are engaged in what was once routine service to the poetry community: translation, book reviews, editing magazines, essays on poetry, the introduction of other—historical or foreign—work, discoveries of neglected masters, new readings of well-known texts, poetry readings where one reads the work of others: any sort of literary context in which to locate themselves.

The only context is the political constituency, the affiliation most easily recognizable for the grants-giving panels: ethnic group, region, gender, sexual (but not culinary or sartorial) preference. In the population explosion of poets, one is only a "poet" at the end of a long line of qualifiers. Hart Crane is now a gay WASP Ohioan.

At a conference on "The Role of Poetry in Society," one session is titled "Poetry Now." For two and a half hours, the poets talk only of teaching.

At any poetry reading, the poet is about to begin a poem, dips her/his head, pauses, smiles to his/her self, looks up, and makes a lightly witty remark. A crowd-pleaser. After all, that identical gesture elected Reagan.

The translations of Shakespeare into Swahili done by President Julius Nyerere of Tanzania set off a renaissance of writing in a language many writers had forsaken for English.

Our President was once asked what was the most important book he had ever read. The answer was *War and Peace*. Tolstoy's words hadn't made much of an impression, but the impossible length of the book was a challenge. The young George Bush was determined to finish it—and, by George, he did.

Yes, there have been instances of successful government patronage of the arts: among others in this century, the Soviet Union in the first years after the Revolution, Mexico in the 1920s and early 1930s under the mass education programs of José Vasconcelos, the U.S. in the Depression under Roosevelt. But these were dependent on two factors. First, the artists and writers were generally enthusiastic about the governments—or at least certain national policies—that were supporting them: there was an overwhelming sense of working for the common good. Second, in all three cases the government was not merely handing out money but getting something in return. This was evident materially: murals on public buildings, outdoor sculpture, public-service posters, postage stamp designs, free concerts, photographs and films documenting farms and industries and the plight of the poor, musical and political theater groups giving free performances in the provinces, government publications written by serious writers, and so on. These works also served the reigning ideologies, directly and indirectly, without necessarily compromising the artist: Soviet Constructivism as the new design for the new world; the Mexican rediscovery and celebration of its pre-Columbian past and indigenous present creating an historical foundation for its revolutionary populism; the American emphasis on realism and documentation as the only way to tell the tale of the time. Some of these works never rose above propaganda, many are among the best of their societies.

Successful government patronage depends, above all, on commissioned work: things which otherwise would not have been produced and, moreover, which are *not for sale*. At the NEA, grants are given for work which goes into the marketplace—however little money there may be in specific markets—and, at the individual level, for work that will be created regardless of whether a grant is received. (And of course the bulk of government money goes to the "arts administrators," experts in attractive proposal packaging, whose first priority is finding the "funding" for their own salaries.)

To receive a grant from the NEA, a poet must now sign two statements:

One, that the recipient "will not engage in the unlawful manufacture, distribution, dispensation, possession, or use of a controlled substance in conducting any activity with the grant."

Two—the provision insisted upon by the ideologue Jesse Helms and passed by a cowardly Senate—that the money will not be used to "promote, disseminate, or produce obscene or indecent materials, including but not limited to depictions of sado-masochism, homoeroticism, the exploitation of children, or individuals engaged in sex acts; or material which denigrates the objects or beliefs of the adherents of a particular religion or nonreligion; or material which denigrates, debases, or reviles a person, group, or class of citizens on the basis of race, creed, sex, handicap, age, or national origin."

Although both provisions are directly applicable to much of world literature, as far as I know, not a single poet has not signed.

It was once a badge of honor for the avant-garde to work in such a way that no one would give you money for it. Now, they dutifully line up and, if rejected, cry "censorship"—the American image of censorship at the end of a century that has murdered hundreds and imprisoned thousands of writers.

Every poet insists that teaching is only a living—the pay good, the hours short—which has no effect on the writing. Every poet insists that *my* work is not compromised by taking money from an otherwise cruel and murderous government which she or he privately despises.

In the pages of the last leftist (leftish) magazines like *The Nation,* filling the small spaces at the end of the terrifying and disheartening articles, they publish their anecdotes of last summer in Maine.

[September 1989]

CHINA IS HERE

A few weeks ago magazines in sixteen countries, led by *Actuel* in France, published a six-page supplement entirely in Chinese. Copying the format of the official Party organ, the *People's Daily*, the supplement contained articles and information concerning the Democracy Movement in China: news of arrests and executions, accounts of the Tiananmen Square massacre, satires, cartoons, and statements by student leaders. These were accompanied by a list of 6,500 fax numbers in the People's Republic. Readers were asked to fax copies of the supplement to any of the numbers, chosen at random. This "fax-in"—a fortuitous combination of Marshall McLuhan, John Cage, the Yippies, and the old propaganda tactic of dropping leaflets from an airplane— has been a great annoyance and a huge success. Armed guards have been posted at fax machines in Beijing, and the Chinese government has already lodged formal protests in France and Venezuela, where the newspaper *Exceso* was a participant.

It is the latest piece of street theater in a drama that has unfolded not only in Beijing, Chengdu, and other Chinese cities, but across the international airwaves and telephone lines. The Chinese Democracy Movement has been, in many ways, the first student protest to occur in the global village.

Last spring, the protesters in Tiananmen Square regularly received the locally censored news reports about themselves via fax from Chinese students in the U.S. and Europe. In the U.S., one could turn on the 24-hour news channel CNN at any moment to watch events in the Square as they bounced off the television satellites, and every evening the ABC news program "Nightline" featured student leaders in Beijing being interviewed "live" by Ted Koppel in Washington. For a few weeks Tiananmen Square regained its traditional place in Chinese thought: it became, again, the center of the earth.

Given this exposure, and the tremendous support both from abroad and among the Chinese people, it seemed impossible at the time that the government would—or would even be able to— suppress the movement. The students who appeared on American television were wildly optimistic and—given the history of China—reckless in their harsh criticism and frank statements. Many of those seen and heard last spring are now dead, disappeared, or in prison.

Some, however, have managed to escape, and eight of them recently appeared in New York in an extraordinary series of panel discussions and poetry readings sponsored by the PEN American Center. The three evenings, like a Russian novel, were hot with the classic conflicts of old and young, insiders and outsiders, revolutionaries and aesthetes, those who proclaimed the birth of an entirely new world and those who saw the recurrence of an ancient pattern.

The long view was epitomized by the historian Jonathan Spence, who began one of the evenings by placing the recent events in four historical contexts. First, a continuing tradition of intellectual protest in China, which is at least as old as Confucius, and stems from the Confucian ideal that those who are educated have a moral obligation to speak out against injustice. Second, a tradition of student protest, which began at the end of the Empire with the anti-Japanese and nationalist movements in 1898, 1919, 1926, and 1935—an inversion of the traditional Confucian wisdom that the young would only be worth listening to when they had attained education and maturity—and which had accelerated in the last thirteen years in a series of major demonstrations in 1976, 1978, 1986, and now 1989. Third, a tradition of repression by the government, as ancient as the Empire itself, due to the absence of the concept of a loyal opposition— opposition in China having always been seen as a subversion to be eliminated. And fourth, a tradition, since the 16th century, of eagerly desiring the technology of the West while simultaneously believing that Western ideas and values will corrupt the soul of China. In Spence's words, "an absolute determination by the Chinese government to stop the adaptation of technology from being linked to the civil life of the society as a whole."

The critic Su Wei, who had spent ten years in forced labor in the countryside during the Cultural Revolution, contradicted Spence's historical perspective by emphasizing the differences between traditional Chinese culture and what he called Chinese "Socialist-Communist Party culture," which had replaced Confucian loyalty to one's family with adherence to the various Party factions. The Party had remained in power, he said, by dismissing "all the talented, open-minded, outstanding intellectuals," retaining only "the most moronic and mediocre," by keeping the nation in "perpetual imbalance" (instituting reforms and then quickly repressing them), and by lies, threats, and a kind of enforced amnesia—the latter most recently exemplified by the official denial of the massacre.

Spence replied that while Party culture may be more thorough than the imperial society, "fundamental patterns of behavior" had not changed and, in fact, that it was the "superficiality" of the Communist government—its inability to enact a truly radical reformation of Chinese society—that had remained its essential failure. In that he was joined by the Tiananmen student leaders, Shen Tong and Wuer Kaixi, who agreed that Chinese history was of a single piece ("a feudalistic, despotic, and closed culture which has lasted for 5,000 years"). Now, at the end of these millennia, they described themselves as part of a "lost and disoriented" generation devoted to the "single-minded pursuit of individuality." According to Wuer: "The favorite word among the youth in China is 'No.'"

That "No" echoed across the conversations. Bei Dao—the best-known of the new poets and, at forty, something of an elder statesman for the protesters—recalled that, earlier in the day, as they strolled through Chinatown, the poet Duo Duo had remarked that the only thing left of Chinese civilization is its food. The painter Ai Weiwei said bluntly: "I think it's very funny that we should be discussing Chinese culture, because, for me, in modern-day China there is no culture." Wuer pointed out that the song most popular among Chinese youth is called "I Have

Absolutely Nothing." Bei Dao's most famous poem states: "Let me tell you, world, / I—do—not—believe!"

It was evident, listening to them, that the Democracy Movement, contrary to its portrayal in the press, had little to do with politics at all—other than, as the cultural historian Perry Link pointed out, a traditional protest against the corruption of the bureaucrats (which is a major theme of Ming Dynasty novels). Rather it was, like the Western student protests of the late 1960s, a cultural revolt: a cult of the individual, a cult of hedonism, a refusal to become yet another drone in the work force and in society. Wuer divided the students into four groups: those who are attempting to pass the examination required to study abroad; those who play mah-jong all day; those who hang out at the discos; and those who try to pick up tourists. Shen Tong emphasized the sexual awakening of the students. [China may have produced a billion people, but it apparently has been dreary for the previous generations. A recent Kinsey-style report claims that the average duration of foreplay in the country is one minute.] Both frequently mentioned that the greatest influences on the movement were pop songs and, above all, poetry.

For those of us accustomed to poetry's current role in the West as a monastic art, it is startling to realize its importance to the Chinese youth, both as the conscience of their generation and as a spur toward change. It began in the 1970s with the "Obscure Poets" (as they were labeled by the Establishment in the "Anti-Spiritual Pollution" campaign), who rejected socialist realism, with its glorifications of mass production and revolutionary heroes, in favor of a simple subjective lyricism: an impressionistic, imagistic, sometimes surrealistic poetry, usually written in the first person. The models, for these poets and the 1980s generation, are all Western: the Romantics, Rimbaud, Baudelaire, Blake, Mandelstam, Dylan Thomas, Sylvia Plath. Not surprisingly, all of these were perceived as "outsiders" to their societies, and the Chinese poets similarly have tended to adopt Bohemian personae to match their writings. (The poet Bei Ling commented that "the personalities of the poets have become increasingly strange: they are all either masochistic or sadistic.")

After two centuries of Romanticism, and weary now with the incessant narcissism of contemporary writers, it is impossible for us to imagine the subversive effect of the word "I" on a collectivist society, particularly one that has suffered the brutalities of the Cultural Revolution. Poets like Bei Dao and Duo Duo are cultural icons, China's pop stars, and Duo Duo claimed, probably wildly, that there are now some 600,000 poets in China. (Demographically, one fourth of the world's poets *should* be Chinese.) They are published in thousands of little magazines and pamphlets in every city, all of them outside the official channels. (Duo Duo wryly remarked that the poets who are published in the official journals are those who failed in the underground.)

What these poets and other writers should be writing, after the Tiananmen massacre, became the subject of debate between Zhang Xinxin, a novelist, and Li Tuo, an academic and literary critic. Zhang—unconsciously echoing Brecht's "What times are these, when to talk about trees is a crime?"—claimed that writers should, at least temporarily, as she has done, suspend "literary" writing for the elite in favor of journalism that would inform the people of what was occurring. Li Tuo, although he had left his position to participate in the demonstrations, echoed the other side of this ancient debate, maintaining that writers should write what they must write: "When Goethe was alive the German peasants also had a very hard life, but Goethe did not go and become a journalist; instead he wrote *Faust*."

It is, of course, a debate that has kept students up all night for decades. Bei Dao, however, brought a local twist to the discussion: "In the past ten years, I've found myself in this very strange and almost absurd situation of trying to do something, but accomplishing the exact opposite. The harder I tried to stay away from politics, the deeper I sank into it." That is, in a totally politicized society, to talk about trees becomes the most political act of all.

Although the writers frequently spoke of rescuing Chinese civilization, it was remarkable that, in the course of the discussions, there was only one reference (and that one inaccurate) to any person or moment in classical Chinese history. Other than their image of Mao as the truly Last Emperor, it was as though the 5,000 years before 1949 had never existed. Li Tuo, the most erudite of the group, cited Melville, Hawthorne, Foucault, Derrida, Goethe, Joyce—but not a single writer from the Chinese past.

Talking later with Bei Dao and Duo Duo, we spent hours circling around this question. Both poets readily admitted that all of their influences had come from the West. For Duo Duo, Chinese civilization is over: "Look at me," he said, pointing to his blue jeans and leather jacket, "there's nothing Chinese about me!" [I thought of, but did not mention, the thousands of students sitting-in outside of Deng Xiaoping's residence in May: They had spontaneously arranged themselves in groups that were cordoned-off; to go from one area to another, one needed a pass. It was exactly the way the Forbidden City had been organized in Imperial times.] Bei Dao pointed out that Western civilization was an amalgam of various cultures—Egyptian, Hebrew, Greek, Arabic, as well as its indigenous peoples—whereas China had evolved, with the exception of the introduction of Buddhism from India—he didn't mention the importation of Marxism-Leninism—largely in isolation, and the end of that isolation was long overdue. For both poets, the only possible salvation of China will come from Western ideas. Duo Duo echoed the program of the 1919 May Fourth Movement, Western "science and rationality"—though it is clear from his poetry that what he personally has discovered is art and Western irrationality. Bei Dao, it seems, still holds to some sort of synthesis of East and West.

I attempted, unsuccessfully, to bring up the modernist model: that in the 20th century the "revolution of the word" consisted not only of radical forms of writing and the promotion of the members of the group, but also a recovery of unknown, forgotten, or heterodox traditions from the past: Pound's Chinese, Provençal, and Anglo-Saxon; Eliot's rediscovery of the Metaphysicals; the Surrealists' promotion of Sade and Fourier, African, Oceanic, and pre-Columbian art; and so on. In Chinese poetry the "canon" has remained largely unchanged for centuries (although Mao erased certain figures). If a major revision is to occur, one would imagine that these are precisely the poets to do it. But this seems, for the moment, unlikely: in disgust with the present, they have obliterated the past. (And, unlike their parents and grandparents, they have no Utopian future.)

Both poets are suffering in their exiles: Duo Duo in London; Bei Dao, separated from his wife and child, who have not been permitted to leave, in various Northern European countries. Bei Dao remarked, somewhat bitterly, that the Eastern European writers in exile are at least still in the West, in their "larger cultural context." And yet the exile of these poets, along with the thousands of other Chinese, may turn out to be as illuminating as it is painful. Despite their obsession with the West, their knowledge of it is extremely haphazard, based on whatever flotsam and jetsam happened to wash up on their shore. In exile, at least, they are adrift in a sea of books, people, and ideas.

Listening to the students and writers, it is obvious that, no matter how long the geriatric authorities manage to hold on to their power, the tide is irreversible. Tens of thousands of Chinese have now studied abroad; hundreds of thousands of them have written poetry and have experienced the thrill of self-expression. (Regardless of their literary worth, these acts of writing are a form of resistance.) Millions have seen the clothes and gadgets on the tourists who have flooded China in the last fifteen years. Hundreds of millions more now watch imported programs on television every day, full of subversive messages about the material lives of ordinary people in the West. No one, at least in the cities, is unaware of the consumer paradises Chinese people themselves have created in Taiwan and Hong Kong. How can they ever again submit to a life of self-sacrifice to country and Party—particularly the young, who have no memory of the hardships (the famines, the Japanese occupation) that led to the Party's initial success? In the end, blue jeans and Walkmans have proved to be more powerful than all the weapons and rhetoric of the century's competing ideologies.

[November 1989]

THE CAMERA PEOPLE

There is a tribe, known as the Ethnographic Filmmakers, who believe they are invisible. They enter a room where a feast is being celebrated, or the sick cured, or the dead mourned, and, though weighted down with odd machines entangled with wires, imagine they are unnoticed—or, at most, merely glanced at, quickly ignored, later forgotten.

Outsiders know little of them, for their homes are hidden in the partially uncharted rain forests of the Documentary. Like other Documentarians, they survive by hunting and gathering information. Unlike others of their filmic group, most prefer to consume it raw.

Their culture is unique in that wisdom, among them, is not passed down from generation to generation: they must discover for themselves what their ancestors knew. They have little communication with the rest of the forest, and are slow to adapt to technical innovations. Their handicrafts are rarely traded, and are used almost exclusively among themselves. Produced in great quantities, the excess must be stored in large archives.

They worship a terrifying deity known as Reality, whose eternal enemy is its evil twin, Art. They believe that to remain vigilant against this evil, one must devote oneself to a set of practices known as Science. Their cosmology, however, is unstable: for decades they have fought bitterly among themselves as to the nature of their god and how best to serve him. They accuse each other of being secret followers of Art; the worst insult in their language is "aesthete."

Ethnos, "a people"; *graphe,* "a writing, a drawing, a representation." Ethnographic film, then: "a representation on film of a people." A definition without limit, a process with unlimited possibility, an artifact with unlimited variation. But nearly a hundred years of practice have considerably narrowed the range of subjects and the forms of representation. Depending on one's perspective, ethnographic film has become either a subgenre of the documentary or a specialized branch of anthropology, and it teems with contention at the margins of both.

Cinema, like photography sixty years before, begins by making the familiar strange: In 1895 the citizens of La Ciotat observed the arrival of a train with indifference, but those who watched Louis Lumière's version of the event, *L'Arrivée d'un Train en Gare,* reportedly dove under their seats in terror. In one sense, this was the purest nonfiction film, the least compromised representation of "reality": the passengers walking blankly by Lumière's camera, not knowing that they are being filmed—how could they know?—are the first and, with a few exceptions, the last filmed people who were not actors, self-conscious participants in the filmmaking. In another sense, the film was pure fiction: like Magritte's pipe, the audience in their panic had intuitively grasped that *This is not a train.*

Recapitulating photography, film's second act was to make the strange familiar. In the same year as Lumière's thrilling train, Félix-Louis Regnault went to the West Africa Exposition in Paris to film a Wolof woman making a ceramic pot. It is Regnault, however, not Lumière, who is considered the first ethnographic filmmaker. The reason is obvious: the "people" represented by ethnography are always somebody else. We, the urban white people, held until recently the film technology and the "scientific" methodology to record and analyze *them:* the non-Westerners and a few remote white groups. Moreover, according to our myth of the Golden Age, *they* lived in societies which had evolved untold ages ago and had remained in suspended animation until their contact with, and contamination by *us.* Ethnographic filmmaking began, and continues as, a salvage operation, as Franz Boas described anthropology. Film, said Regnault, "preserves forever all human behaviors for the needs of our studies." Oblivious to such hyperbole (and formaldehyde), Emilie de Brigard, an historian of the genre, writes that this is the "essential function" of ethnographic film, that it remains "unchanged today."

Where travelers had gone to collect adventures, missionaries to collect souls, anthropologists to collect data, and settlers to collect riches, filmmakers were soon setting out to collect and preserve human behaviors: the only good Indian was a filmed Indian. Within a few years of Regnault's first effort, anthropologists were taking film cameras into the field for their studies, and movie companies were sending crews to strange locales for popular entertainment. It is a curiosity of that era that the two polar allegorical figures in the history of early cinema, the Lumières ("Realism") and the Méliès ("Fantasy") were both engaged in shooting such exotica.

By the mid-1920s, the representation of other people had evolved into three genres. At one extreme, the anthropological film, largely concerned, as it is today, with recording a single aspect of a culture (a ritual, the preparation of a food, the making of a utilitarian or sacred object) or attempting some sort of inventory. At the other, the fictional romance featuring indigenous people, such as the Méliès' *Loved by a Maori Chieftainess* (1913), shot in New Zealand and now lost, or Edward Curtis' *In the Land of the Head-Hunters* (1914), made among the Kwakiutl. Somewhere in-between was a genre inadvertently named by John Grierson in a 1926 review of Robert Flaherty's second film: "Of course, *Moana*, being a visual account of events in the daily life of a Polynesian youth and his family, has documentary value."

Documentum, "an example, a proof, a lesson." Grierson's comment was not inaccurate, but there are few cases where it would not be applicable. Fiction, non-fiction, highbrow and low: much of what any of us knows of much of the world comes from film: the daily operations of institutions like the police or the army or the prisons or the courts, life on board a submarine, how pickpockets work the Paris métro, how Southern California teenagers mate. Filling the frame of every film, no matter how "fictional," is an endless documentation of its contemporary life: a documentation that becomes most apparent with geographical or chronological distance. A Mack Sennett two-reeler is, for us now, much more than a pie in the face: it is long johns and cranked autos, plump women in impossible bathing costumes, and the implicit Middle American xenophobia in the figure of the crazed mustachioed immigrant anarchist. The ditziest Hollywood production bears a subversive documentary message for viewers in China or Chad: this is what ordinary people in the U.S. have in their houses, this is what they have in their refrigerators. Even the most fantastical films "document" their cultures: *Nosferatu* and *The Cabinet of Dr. Caligari* are inextricable from Weimar Germany, Steven Spielberg from Reagan America. Above all—and particularly in the United States—many of the greatest works of the imagination begin with the premise that a universe is revealed in the luminous facts of ordinary life. The most extreme case is America's greatest novel: a cosmology derived from the meticulous details, framed in a slight narrative, of an unheroic, low-caste profession that was considered disgusting at the time: the sea-going blubber-renderers of *Moby-Dick*.

But in film it is precisely the fuzzy border between "documentary value" and "documentation" (a proof that is independently verifiable) that has led so many filmmakers and critics into acrimonious philosophical debate and methodological civil wars. *Moana* (1926) is a case in point: the work of a revered totemic ancestor in both the documentary and ethnographic lineages. Shot on the Samoan island of Savaii—"the one island where the people still retain the spirit and nobility of their race"—the film is subtitled *A Romance of the Golden Age*. Moana is played by a Samoan named Ta'avale; his "family" was cast from villagers, based on their looks. They are dressed in costumes that had long since been replaced by Western clothes, their hair is done in similarly archaic, "authentic" styles, and the women, almost needless to say, have been returned to their bare-breasted beauty.

There are scenes of "documentary value": gathering taro roots, setting a trap for a wild boar, fishing with spears in the incredibly limpid water, making a dress from mulberry bark. But to introduce what he called "conflict" into this portrayal of an utterly idyllic life, Flaherty paid Ta'avale to undergo a painful ritual tattooing which had dropped out of practice a few generations before. (The titles read: "There is a rite through which every Polynesian must pass to win the right to call himself a man. Through this pattern of the flesh, to you perhaps no more than cruel, useless ornament, the Samoan wins the dignity, the character and the fiber which keeps his race alive.") It is the conceit of the film that all we have seen so far "has been preparation for the great event": the climatic scene that intercuts the tattooing, frenetic dancing, and an otherwise unexplained "witch woman." (Moana's tattoo, unfortunately, is visible in the first minute of the film.)

In *Nanook of the North: A Story of Life and Love in the Actual Arctic* (1922) the "chief of the Itiumuits, the great hunter Nanook, famous through all Ungara" is played by an Eskimo named Allakariallak. (The character's name seems to be all-purpose: Flaherty planned to make a movie of the Acoma Indians of the Southwest called *Nanook of the Desert*.) The film is also set in the past, without noting the fact. The harpoons with which these "fearless, lovable, happy-go-lucky Eskimos" hunt walruses had long given way to rifles, and, in that crowd-pleasing scene, the gramophone record which Nanook bites was already a familiar item. Other scenes are transparently staged: the seal with which Nanook struggles (and pulls out of the ice-hole twice) in the famous sequence is obviously Dead on Arrival; the unmenacing "wild wolf" is tugging at a leash; and Nanook's family looks pretty chilly pretending to sleep in the half-igloo Flaherty had ordered constructed for sufficient light and his bulky camera. Again, in *Man of Aran* (1934), Flaherty revived customs extinct for as much as a hundred years, including the shark hunts that are the heart of the film. And again, he was sloppy with details: the cottages, lit by shark-oil lamps, clearly have electric wires running from roof to roof.

Flaherty is well-known for the remark, "Sometimes you have to lie. One often has to distort a thing to catch its true spirit." And his longtime assistant, Helen Van Dongen, wrote: "To me

Flaherty is *not* a documentarian; he makes it all up." But he didn't have to: the struggle against hunger in the Arctic persisted whether the Eskimos carried harpoons or rifles ("Nanook" later died of starvation on a hunt); the Aran Islanders continued to confront a raging sea even if electricity had replaced shark oil as their source of light; and "conflict" in idyllic Samoa was plain enough at the time in the social tensions caused by the missionaries, merchants, and British colonial administrators—which is the theme of an on-location though strictly Hollywood romance only two years later, W. S. Van Dyke's *White Shadows in the South Seas* (1928), where "the last remnants of an earthly paradise . . . from the morning of civilization" is turned into a squalid honky-tonk.

Flaherty, unlike many others to come, spent long periods of time living in the communities he was planning to film. (After ten years in the Arctic, exploring for mineral ore deposits and making home movies, he persuaded the fur company Revillon Frères to finance *Nanook* as a kind of feature-length commercial.) He was the first to screen the daily rushes for the principals, for their comments—a participatory filmmaking that would be abandoned until Jean Rouch revived the practice in the 1950s. Many of his scenes remain astonishingly beautiful, particularly the still-unparalleled shots of the sea crashing against the cliffs, bouncing the canoes and kayaks, exploding through blow-holes (perhaps Flaherty was greater as an oceanographic filmmaker than as an ethnographic one). And, above all, his image of humanness, particularly in *Nanook* and *Man of Aran*—the lone individual and the small community valiantly overcoming the brutalities of their environment—has had universal appeal in a century most notable for the victimization of its masses. [An appeal that even extended to the victimizers: Mussolini gave *Man of Aran* a prize, and Goebbels declared that it exemplified the virtue and spirit of fortitude that Hitler wanted the German people to possess. (Churchill's favorite films were the Marx Brothers', which may have affected the outcome of the war.) It must be recognized, however, that in certain ethnographic films, the emphasis on the courageous individual, the "wisdom of the folk," and the erotic-

ization of the pure "savage" human body is equally characteristic
of Fascist art. It's a small leap from Leni Riefenstahl's *Olympiad* to
her *Last of the Nuba,* particularly in the former's portrayal of
Jesse Owens.] But in the end, Flaherty belongs most exactly to
the popular travelogues and "romances" of the silent era, shot on
location with native actors—though his films were less stylized,
less narrative, and more naturalistic.

With the advent of sound, the expense and the size of the
equipment forced most filmmakers to move the exotic to the
backlot, and, far more than Flaherty, make it all up. [Richard
Leacock was fond of quoting an old Hollywood manual on light-
ing: "When shooting Westerns, use real Indians if possible; but if
Indians are not available, use Hungarians."] The career of Mer-
ian Cooper and Ernest Schoedsack is exemplary: They began
with *Grass* (1925) a stirring account of the annual migration by
50,000 Bakhtyari shepherds across the Zardeh Kuh mountains
of Turkey and Persia. [It is, by the way, probably the only documentary film to end with an actual document: a notarized letter
by the British consul in Teheran stating that the filmmakers were
indeed the first foreigners to make the journey.] From Persia
they went to Siam to film *Chang* (1927), an action-adventure
featuring Lao hill people "who have never seen a motion pic-
ture" and "wild beasts who have never feared a rifle." By 1933,
Cooper and Schoedsack were directing black-faced extras in
their ritual worship of King Kong.

The Depression and the Second World War effectively
stopped most ethnographic film production. In 1958, the genre
revived with the most successful film of its kind since *Nanook,*
and one cast strictly in the Flaherty mold: John Marshall's *The
Hunters.* Like Flaherty, Marshall had not been trained as an ethnographer, but had spent years living with the people he filmed,
the !Kung Bushmen of the Kalahari Desert in southern Africa.
Like *Nanook* and *Man of Aran,* the film portrays courageous
men—it is always men in these films—surviving in a harsh environment: the !Kung are a "quiet people" engaged in a "ceaseless
struggle" for food in a "bitter land indeed where all the trees

have thorns." Rather than one great hunter, *The Hunters* has four—though they are indistinguishable—whom it follows on a hunt that ends with the killing of a giraffe.

Like Flaherty, Marshall is impossibly sloppy. Though the hunt, for some reason, is supposed to take place over thirteen consecutive days, it is clearly a pastiche of footage taken over many years. Not only does the number of giraffes in the herd they are tracking (seen in long shots) keep changing, the protagonists themselves are not always the same. And, as anthropologists have pointed out, !Kung subsistence was based more on gathering than hunting and, at the time, they had plenty of food. (They began to face starvation when the South African government put them on reservations.)

The film is sustained by continual narration. At times the narrator is a crafty insider ("Kaycho water is always brackish this time of year"; the kudus—a kind of antelope—are "more restless than usual"; and so on). At other times, Marshall takes the Voice of God, familiar in most documentaries since the invention of sound, to new heights. Not only does he tell us what the men are thinking—what one critic has wittily called the telepathic fallacy—we even learn the thoughts and feelings of the wounded giraffe. ("She traveled in an open country with a singleness of mind." Later, she is "troubled," "too dazed to care," and "no longer has her predicament clearly in mind.") Worst of all, God has been reading Hemingway: "He found the dung of a kudu. A kudu is a big animal. A kudu would be ample meat to bring home." The machismo of such spoken prose becomes manifest when the final killing of the female giraffe is described in terms of gang rape: The men "exhausted their spears and spent their strength upon her."

The film ends elevating this false narrative into myth: "And old men remembered. And young men listened. And so the story of the hunt was told." But the heroic exploits incessantly emphasized by the narrator are contradicted by what we are actually seeing in the film. They really are lousy hunters. The one kudu they manage to kill (with an utterly unheroic steel trap) is eaten by vultures and hyenas; only the bones are left for the men to rapaciously gnaw. (What, meanwhile, was the film crew eating?) And when the giraffe (also wounded by a trap) is finally cornered and dying, the men keep throwing their spears and missing. No doubt this is what hunting is actually like: Why then should Marshall insist, in his narration, that these "real" people are as unerring as some Hollywood white rajah of the jungle?

And yet filmmaker David MacDougall, otherwise quite strict about these matters, articulates the general opinion: *The Hunters* is "one of the few true ethnographic films we have," "a case of synthesis put to the service of truth."

The other celebrated ethnographic film of the era, Robert Gardner's *Dead Birds* (1963), employs many of Flaherty's conventions to produce a kind of anti-*Nanook:* a film that, perhaps inadvertently, is far from ennobling. Shot among the Dani, a previously little-documented group in Western New Guinea, the film is a narrative—based, like Flaherty, on a series of archetypal anecdotes rather than the full-blown dramatic structure and developed characterizations of a "plot"—about a warrior, Weyak, and a small boy, Pua. (The boy-figure in *Moana* is named Pe'a.) The characters do not speak; their actions (and, like *The Hunters,* thoughts) are conveyed to us by a continual narration, spoken by Gardner. Perhaps uniquely in ethnographic films, the narration is delivered in a nervous, unnaturally rapid speech: an edginess that considerably adds to the film's dramatic tensions.

Its unforgettable opening clearly announces some sort of allegory: a very long pan of a hawk flying over the treetops, and the spoken words: "There is a fable told by a mountain people living in the ancient highlands of New Guinea . . ." [It is a convention of the genre: the people are remote and as timeless as geography, but will be revealed to be, in some way, just like us. *Grass* opens by promising us the "Forgotten People" who will unlock the "secrets of our own past." *Nanook* opens by taking us to "mysterious barren lands" that, conversely, are "a little kingdom—nearly as large as England."] The fable is the story of the origin of human mortality: a race between a bird and a snake to determine whether people would die like birds or shed their skins and live forever like snakes. Needless to say, the bird won, and *Dead Birds,* in the Flaherty tradition of portraying man against the odds, was apparently intended as a portrayal of one culture's response to the universal destiny. Gardner writes: "I saw the Dani People, feathered and fluttering men and women, as enjoying the fate of all men and women. They dressed their lives with plumage, but faced as certain death as the rest of us drabber souls. The film attempts to say something about how we all, as humans, meet our animal fate."

What the film actually shows is something quite different. With the exception of one quite powerful funeral scene, *Dead Birds* is not concerned with the effects of human destiny—rites, mourning, grief—but rather its provocation. The Dani were perhaps the last people on earth to engage in a rigidly codified ritual war. (One which finally was ended by the local "authorities" shortly after the film was made.) The men of neighboring villages, separated only by their gardens and a strip of no man's land, would regularly adorn themselves and gather on a battlefield, fighting (theoretically) until there was one fatal casualty. Revenge for that death would provoke the next battle, and so on forever. An endless vendetta war in a land with plenty of food and no particular differences between the villages; where no territory or plunder was captured; with no mass killings and no deviation from the rules.

In fact—or at least according to the film—revenge was rarely achieved on the battlefield. In the battles themselves there is a great deal of back and forth feints and threats, but no hand-to-hand combat; wounds are mainly inflicted haphazardly in the shower of arrows. The two murders in the film, one for each side, occur when a group of men accidentally comes across someone from the other side: a small boy who wandered off, a man trying to steal a pig at night.

A continual, senseless war; battles where the two sides engage in menacing rhetoric but do relatively little harm; covert killings; a no man's land lined with tall watchtowers; daily life in a state of permanent dread. The allegorical import of *Dead Birds* must have been obvious to its viewers in 1963, when the Berlin Wall was still new. The film is hardly a meditation on death at all: if it were it would have presented Dani who had died from childbirth, sickness, accidents, age. Rather it is a feathered and fluttering reenactment of the Cold War that was being prolonged and endured at the time by the drab souls of East and West.

After this, his first film, Gardner would abandon the Flaherty anecdotal narrative of the hunter/warrior, both epitome and paragon of his people, the boy who wishes to emulate him, and the Western bard who sings his praises. In *Dead Birds,* Weyak is introduced by a shot of his hands (Flaherty: "Simply in the beautiful movement of a hand the whole story of a race can be revealed"), Pua by his reflection in a puddle. In the later films, Gardner would devolve an ethnographic cinema based entirely on such telling details and oblique images, films that would pose little difficuty to general audiences accustomed to foreign imports, but which the scientists would find incomprehensible.

In the 1950s ethnographic film became an academic discipline with the usual array of specialist practitioners, pedagogues, and critics. It has always seen itself as besieged on two sides. On one flank, the anthropologists whose conception of a representation of a people has always emphasized the written meaning of *graphe*—and moreover the fixed singularity of the *mono*-graph. (As recently as 1988, filmmaker Timothy Asch was complaining that they "have shown little interest in the potential use of ethnographic film.") On the other flank, the aesthetes, or as Margaret Mead put it: "There's a bunch of filmmakers now that are saying 'It should be art' and wrecking everything we're trying to do."

To prove their mettle to the anthropologists, ethnographic filmmakers have tended to adopt a more-scientific-than-thou attitude. Asch, in a scary comment, writes, "The camera can be to the anthropologist what the telescope is to the astronomer or what the microscope is to the biologist"—which assumes that the matter on the other side of the ethnographic lens is as imperturbable as galaxies or amoebae. Mead, who shot a great deal of footage in Bali in the 1930s with Gregory Bateson, believed that "objective" filming would replace "subjective" field notes, an idea picked up by David MacDougall who, speaking for the reception side, writes that film speaks "directly to the audience, without the coding and decoding inevitable with written language," a notion disproved by the second screening of Lumière's train. And the main textbook in the field, Karl Heider's *Ethnographic Film* (1976), is an attempt to set "standards" and create a "rational, explicit methodology" for the discipline.

Just what some of them have in mind was first articulated by Mead:

> Finally, the oft-repeated argument that all recording and filming is selective, that none of it is objective, has to be dealt with summarily. If tape recorder, camera, or video is set up and left in the same place, large batches of material can be collected without the intervention of the filmmaker or ethnographer and without the continuous self-consciousness of those who are being observed. The camera or tape recorder that stays in one spot, that is not tuned, wound, refocused, or visibly loaded, does become part of the background scene, and what it records did happen.

Such a utopian mechanism—a panopticon with limitless film—has been extrapolated by critic Walter Goldschmidt into a definition of the genre:

> Ethnographic film is film which endeavors to interpret the behavior of people of one culture to persons of another culture by using shots of people doing precisely what they would have been doing if the camera were not there.

The ideal, then, is either a dream of invisibility, or worse, the practice of the surveillance camera. Leaving aside the obvious moral and political questions of surveillance—white folks, as usual, playing God, albeit an immobile one with a single fixed stare—the value of such information could be nothing more than slight. The simplest human events unfold in a tangle of attendant activities, emotions, motivations, responses, and thoughts. One can imagine a !Kung anthropologist attempting to interpret the practices and effects of the American cash economy from footage obtained with the cameras in the local bank.

Such films, amazingly, exist. Among them is *Microcultural Incidents at 10 Zoos* (1971) by Ray Birdwhistell, the inventor of *kinesics,* an analysis of body language. Birdwhistell, who might be one of the dotty anthropologists in Barbara Pym's novels, placed hidden cameras in front of the elephant cages in the zoos of ten countries to discover the national traits of behavior revealed by the way families feed the pachyderms. The resulting film is an illustrated lecture with frame numbers running along the top of the screen, instant replays and freeze frames (including one of a kid being slobbered on by Jumbo), and phrases like "for those interested in proximics" or "note how the father places the peanut in the child's hand." Birdwhistell maintains that "there is enough information in one 4-second loop for a day's class in anthropology." His film—which is based on the assumption that a nation can be represented by a few members—demonstrates that Italians feed themselves while feeding elephants, the British give a slight formal bow, the Japanese keep a respectful distance, the Americans are easily distracted, and so forth—in other words, the kind of ethnographic information we get from television comedians. Birdwhistell, most tellingly, becomes completely flustered when he gets to India: there are too many people milling around to sort out, and they don't seem terribly interested. Despite his expertise of "organized patterning" and "gambits of caretaking," it apparently doesn't occur to him that in many parts of India an elephant is far less exotic than a cocker spaniel.

Birdwhistell may be an extreme case, but there are thousands of hours of such "scientific" ethnographic film, stored in archives like the Encyclopedia Cinematographica in Göttingen, covering probably every remaining tribe on earth, and devoted, in David MacDougall's words, to "rendering faithfully the natural sounds, structure and duration of events"—a description best applied to Andy Warhol's *Sleep.*

In many other disciplines—including, recently, anthropology itself—a "faithful rendering" is recognized as being entirely subject to the vagaries of current style and individual taste. (As fiction and documentary films forever demonstrate, there is nothing more unreal than yesterday's realism.) But ethnographic film, unlike other filmmaking, thinks of itself as science, and a set of rules for the representation of reality has been laid out by Heider: events may not be staged or reconstructed, and must be presented in the order in which they occurred; no soundtrack music; "whole bodies" rather than close-ups; "whole acts" (beginning, middle, and end); "whole people" (emphasis on one or two individuals rather than "faceless masses"); accompanying printed material; and so on.

Adhering to most, but not all, of these dicta is Timothy Asch, one of the most respected of the "scientific" filmmakers. Asch, whose writings display unusual candor, has written: "I was ambitious. I wanted to take film that would be valuable for research as well as for instruction and curriculum development." [Clearly not a dream of making *Citizen Kane*, but then ethnographic filmmakers, with the exceptions of Rouch and Gardner, notably never, in their voluminous writings, mention any films outside of the genre. Apparently they don't go to the movies like the rest of us.]

His best-known project, a series of 21 films of the Yanomano people of the Upper Orinoco, made with the anthropologist Napoleon Chagnon, comes with a "Utilization Chart" which divides cultural research into ten categories and checks off the applicability of each film. It's a grim taxonomy, and weirdly incomplete: Social Organization, Kinship, Political Organization, Conflict, Socialization, Women, Field Work, Ecology & Subsistence, Cosmology & Religion, and Acculturation.

The chart's assumption that human life can be contained by such cubbyholes is identical to the belief that any human activity is most fully represented by long takes, long shots, and "whole bodies." Worse, it assumes an existing structure to which all data must be applied; that which does not is simply excluded:

Chagnon took a 2½ minute sequence of a Yanomano man beating his wife over the head with a piece of firewood. We looked at it together with James V. Neal and his wife, thinking we might include it in our film on genetics. [!] We three men agreed it was too disturbing to show. Mrs. Neal saw this as a typically protective male view and argued that the beating was no worse than the experience of many wives in America. We agree; but we still decided not to use the footage.

Asch and Chagnon's *The Ax Fight* (1975) is an example of messy human life reduced to chunks of explainable phenomena. The film is in five parts. Part 1 is the unedited footage of a fight that suddenly erupts in a Yanomano village; the violence of the scene is matched by the frantic quality of the film, as the hand-held camera wobbles, zooms in, and pans rapidly back and forth to keep up with the action. In Part 2, the screen is black as the filmmakers discuss what happened; Chagnon speculates that it is the reaction to a case of incest. In Part 3, text scrolls up the screen informing us, refreshingly, that the anthropologist was wrong: the fight was the result of a kinship conflict provoked when a woman was ill-treated in a neighboring village; the inevitable kinship charts are then shown. Part 4 replays the original footage with a narrator and pointers identifying the players and their relation to one another. Part 5 presents a polished version of the original, without commentary but edited for narrative continuity. The editing tellingly violates Heider's dictum that events must be presented in the order in which they occurred: as the critic Bill Nichols has pointed out, the original (sequential) footage ends with the wronged woman insulting the men; the narrative version both begins and ends with her, transforming her into a provocateur. (Nichols comments sarcastically, "That's the way women are.")

The opening minutes are an indelible image of community violence, full of unclassifiable data—what filmmaker Jorge Preloran has called the "feel" for a people—a vision of the Yanomano elsewhere unavailable on film. And it is obvious that the sudden outburst and equally sudden resolution of the fight cannot be explained by pointers and kinship charts. One can only imagine the untidy human narrative that would have emerged if the principals and other villagers—who don't speak in the film— were asked to give their versions; if we learned some of their previous history and what happened after the fight. One of the curiosities of ethnographic film, evident to any outsider, is that the strictly scientific films often provide far less information than their reviled "artistic" cousins, which tend to spill over the utilization charts.

Or, more damningly, they provide the same information. There are so many films of the Yanomano that, in Paris in 1978, they could hold a festival of them. These included a number of the Asch-Chagnon films; a French TV documentary; two films from a Yugoslavian TV series on the rain forest; a Canadian film from the TV series *Full Speed to Adventure*, focusing on two Canadian missionaries living with the community; a Japanese TV film; three videos by New York avant-gardist Juan Downey; and unedited footage shot in the early 1960s by a woman gold prospector. The range of what Heider calls "ethnographic understanding" was obviously great: from experienced scientists to newly arrived television crews (only some of whom were accompanied by anthropologists) to the home movies of a passer-by.

There is an account of the festival in *Film Library Quarterly*, written by Jan Sloan. She points out that, despite the diversity of sources, "the actual images were surprisingly similar . . . It is also surprising to note the similarity of information presented in these documentaries. The same limited material is covered in many of the films over and over again . . ."

The recent literary dismantling of written anthropology (by Clifford Geertz, James Clifford, and others) has tried to demonstrate how the sober scientific professionals are no less prone to dubious generalization, manipulation of data, partial explanation, and prevailing ethnocentrism than the enthusiastic amateurs who write accounts of their travels. Similarly, the moment one erases the stylistic differences, the ethnographic differences between a research film and an episode of *Full Speed to Adventure* are less than meets the eye.

The amateurs, in fact, often turn out to be ethnographically richer. Consider the case of an utterly "unscientific" film: *The Nuer* (1970) by Hilary Harris and George Breidenbach, with the assistance of Robert Gardner. Until Gardner's *Forest of Bliss* (1986) this was probably the film most loathed by the professionals. Heider writes: "It is one of the most visually beautiful films ever made . . . But the film is almost without ethnographic integrity. By this I mean that its principles are cinema aesthetic; its framing, cutting, and juxtaposition of images are done without regard for any ethnographic reality." Throughout his book, Heider uses *The Nuer* as the classic example of how not to make an ethnographic film.

The film has no story, little narration, only one brief interview with an individual, no time frame and no events unfolded in their entirety. Most of it consists of rapidly edited shots of extraordinary beauty, accompanied by a soundtrack of local music and sounds and untranslated speech. There are galleries of close-ups—faces, tobacco pipes, jewelry, houses, corrals—and unforgettable sequences of these astonishingly elongated people merely walking through the dust and mist. Much of the film simply looks at the cows that are central to Nuer life: close-ups of cow legs and cow flanks and cow nostrils and cow horns.

Though this is one of the most "aesthetic" films in the genre, it is full of ethnographic information—far more, ironically, than something like *The Ax Fight*. We see and hear what the Nuer look like, what they make, what they eat, what their music sounds like, their leisure activities, body art, architecture, fishing and cattle-herding, local fauna, diseases, rites of exorcism, spiritual possession, and so on. Most of all, as a study of a community based on cattle, it is a startling revelation of the cow. Even an untrained urban eye finds itself immediately differentiating the cows as individuals—much as the Nuer know the personal history of each; a history which, through bride-prices and ritual exchange, is inextricably tangled with their own histories. Moreover, it becomes evident in the course of the film how an entire aesthetic could be derived from the close observation of cattle; how the shapes and textures of the herds are recapitulated in so much of what the Nuer make.

"The final goal, of which an Ethnographer should never lose sight," wrote Malinowski sixty years ago in a famous dictum, now outdated only in its gender specificity, "is, briefly, to grasp the native's point of view, his relation to life, to realize *his* vision of *his* world" (*his* emphasis). Of course the ideal is impossible—who can ever see with another's eyes, even within one's own culture? Yet *The Nuer*, rare among ethnographic films, lets us look closely at that which the Nuer look at, but which most of us do not— moreover seeing, as any of us see anything, not the "whole bodies" but the telling details that set each one apart. It is one of the few instances where ethnographic film presents information that is beyond the capabilities of the written monograph. Not observed and analyzed data: it is a physical and intellectual act of seeing. Neither a recapitulation of a foreign vision nor the first-person expression of the filmmakers, it is, most exactly, an act of translation: a reading of their sensibility, recoded into our (film) language. *The Nuer,* like any film, is a metaphor for the Nuer. Its difference is that it does not pretend to be a mirror.

Bill Nichols has written that the central question of ethnographic film is what to do with the people. This is true enough, but it is a center that must be shared by a parallel question: What to do with the filmmaker. Nanook mugged shamelessly for the camera; such footage ever since has tended to be scissored away, to preserve the illusion that the filmed events are being lived as they're always lived, and not being acted out.

David and Judith MacDougall are notable among the ethnographic filmmakers for making their own presence a central feature of their films. Moreover, they have effectively subverted the authority of the all-knowing narrator not only by allowing the subjects to speak—in the late 1960s they introduced subtitled dialogue to the genre—but also by basing their films on conversation. These take three forms: ordinary conversation among the people as observed and recorded by the filmmakers; conversation among the people on topics initiated by the filmmakers; and dialogue between the filmmakers and the people. That the MacDougalls are talking to their subject matter is radical enough in this corner of the film forest; they also allow themselves to be occasionally glimpsed and, in one startling moment, even show us where they're living during the making of the film. (An anthropologist's house is normally more taboo than the interior of a kiva.) They introduce topics with intertitles written in the first person ("We put the following to Lorang . . ."), and their inter- mittent voice-overs are subjective ("I was sure Lorang's wives were happy together") and sometimes even confessional ("It doesn't feel like we're making progress"). When they don't have certain information or footage, they readily admit it, rather than attempt to patch it over. Most impressively, the films are a *visual* dialogue between the filmmakers and their subjects: at every moment we know exactly where David MacDougall (the camera- man) is standing. And, thanks no doubt to the presence of Judith MacDougall, their films are full of women talking, and talking freely.

In short, they have found seemingly effortless solutions to most of the political and moral dilemmas of ethnographic film. Contrary to Goldschmidt's definition of the genre, the Mac- Dougalls are shooting people doing precisely what they would have been doing with a camera crew there. The procedure, how- ever, does have its limitations: what they are doing is often not terribly interesting.

Their trilogy—*Lorang's Way, A Wife Among Wives,* and *The Wedding Camels* (1978–81)—shot among the Turkana of north- ern Kenya, is a case in point. The films focus on the family of a wealthy man: the first is a portrait of the patriarch, Lorang; the second talks to his wives; the third concerns the negotiations for the marriage of his daughter. The film rarely leaves the family compound, and for nearly six hours we watch and listen to peo- ple largely talking about money and complaining. [Rouch has remarked: "Many recent films of the direct-cinema type are thus spoiled by an incredible regard for the chatting of the people filmed."] Lorang is an Arthur Miller character: the self-made man disgusted by his good-for-nothing sons. But, in the absence of any dramatic catalyst—this being life and not theater—he's a character who goes nowhere: after the first half-hour or so, we only get more of the same. (The wives mainly repeat everything their husband says.) And the film gives us no way to evaluate whether Lorang is more representative of the Turkana or of the universal *nouveau riche*.

In many ways, the trilogy is like an excruciating evening with one's least favorite relatives. There's no doubt it is a precise representation of this particular family, but can it be considered ethnographic, a representation of a people? We actually learn very little about the Turkana besides work, money, and marriage procedures. No one is born, gets sick, or dies in the films; there are no religious ceremonies; very little singing or eating; conflict with the outside world is alluded to, but not shown; although we come to know the compound well, we are never clear where it is or what its neighbors are up to. The family talks and talks . . . As a record, its style is unusually inventive; but it never solves the perennial questions of the genre: When there are no individuals, who speaks for the people? (Usually the wrong man: the narrator). When there is an individual, to what extent can she or he represent the group?

One answer is a multiplicity of voices—voices that echo, enlarge, and especially contradict one another. Certainly it would be possible in six hours of film, but it would undermine the premises of the genre: *They* have typical members. *We* do not. *They* are unusual, but can be comprehended. *We* are usual, but ultimately incomprehensible. *They* are somewhat like us. *We* are not like us. *They* must be represented in the simplest possible way. *We* must be represented with subtle complexity.

Most ethnographic films document a single event—perhaps, as Rouch has suggested, because such events come with their own ready-made *mise en scène*. Such documentation poses a dilemma for the scientists. Written ethnography is based on generalization: the ethnographer's description of, say, how a basket is woven is an amalgam based on watching a hundred baskets being made. Filmed ethnography cannot help but be specific: a unique and idiosyncratic instance of basket-weaving. (Often, the differences between what is seen and what is "usual" will be noted by filmmakers in interviews; but never, as far as I know, in the film itself.) Moreover, the filmed event unravels the image of the "traditional" society on which ethnographic film is based, in a way that a written monograph does not: The endlessly repeated becomes the unrepeatable moment; the timeless is suddenly inserted into history; representation of a people becomes representation of a person; ethnography biography, archetype individual. (And a pastiche, like *The Hunters,* is no way out: it cannot help but be subverted by the expectation of a continuity based on matching shots.)

One solution, not so strangely, is surrealism: a superficial discontinuity revelatory of a profound unity. There are films to be imagined that would self-consciously (unlike *The Hunters*) feature different protagonists at different stages of an event, or the same protagonist in different versions, or one where the protagonists perform in a stylized, "unnatural" reenactment. Films that, to represent a people, would attempt to subvert film's natural tendency to specify individuals. (Would a *Discreet Charm of the Bourgeoisie* or a *Heart of Glass* of ethnographic films be any less stylized, or carry less information, than the currently prevailing modes of realism?)

Surrealism moreover introduced an aesthetic based on chance, improvisation, and the found object—an aesthetic which would seem tailored to the actual conditions of a Westerner making an ethnographic film. Yet the genre has had only one surrealist: ironically, the founder of *cinema verité,* Jean Rouch. (And there's a parallel to be drawn with another surrealist, the master of photojournalism, Henri Cartier-Bresson.) *Jaguar* (shot in the 1950s and released in 1967), to briefly take one example from a massive amount of work, has the improvisatory exuberance of the 1960s French New Wave—it even includes clips from other Rouch films. One can't anticipate what will happen next, as the film follows its three protagonists traveling from Niger to Ghana to find work; some of the adventures—as when one of the men becomes an official photographer for Kwame Nkrumah—even veer into fantasy. Most important, *Jaguar* is the only inventive exploration of non-synch sound in the genre. [Baldwin Spencer had taken an Edison cylinder recorder to Australia in 1901, but these possibilities remained unexplored for fifty years.] Shot silently, the soundtrack (recorded ten years later) features the three men commenting on the action: a nonstop patter of jokes, insults, commentary, and light-heated disagreements that effectively break down the normally unchallenged authority of the single narrator/outsider.

Robert Gardner, in *Deep Hearts* (1978) and *Forest of Bliss* (1987), has adapted another aspect of surrealism to transform the idiosyncratic into the archetypal: he explodes time. By employing the simultaneous time of modern physics, he transforms the linear time of the unrepeatable into the cyclical time of the endlessly repeated. This has been, of course, one of the main projects of the century: through simultaneity—montage, collage, Pound's ideogrammic method—all ages become contemporaneous. It is both a criticism of Western linear time and a bridge to the mythic time which rules most traditional societies. But where the modernists sought to recapture both the formal aspects and the sheer power of so-called "primitive" art and oral epics, Gardner, uniquely, has employed the techniques of modernism to *represent* the tribal other. A cycle has been completed: with Gardner, James Joyce is our entry into Homer.

Deep Hearts is concerned with the annual Garawal ceremony of the Bororo Fulani of Niger. The nomadic groups converge at one spot in the desert, where the young men elaborately make themselves up and, wearing women's dresses, dance for eight days in the sun as the marriageable young women look them over, until one man is selected as the most virtuous and beautiful. According to the few lines of narration in the film, the Bororo consider themselves to be "chosen people" (who doesn't?) but they are threatened by "neighbors, new ideas, disease, and drought." Their combination of "excessive self-regard" and "a fear of losing what they have" makes them "easily prey to envy." So they must bury their hearts within them, for "if a heart is deep no one can see what it contains."

If this group psychological analysis is correct. then the Bororo must remain, particularly to an outsider, unreadable. Everything will remain on the surface, only, at best, inadvertently revealing what is beneath. Gardner's response to this impermeability is to turn it into a dream, a shimmering mirage. Time is scrambled and events keep repeating themselves: men dancing, people arriving, men dancing, preparations for the dance, and so on. Shots of the farewell ceremony, near the end of the film, are followed by a scene we've already seen, near the beginning, of a woman washing her enormous leg bracelets before the dance. Sounds recorded at the dance are played over scenes of preparation for it. There are strange sideways shots of milk being poured from huge bowls that recall the abstract geometries of Moholy-Nagy's films. There are freeze frames and, in one sequence, slow-motion and distortion of the sound. [Though documentary was born out of slow-motion—Edward Muybridge's magic lantern studies of animal locomotion—it remains taboo for ethnographic film, being counter to prevailing notions of realism. Maya Deren's 1947–51 study of voodoo in Haiti, *Divine Horsemen,* exploits both the hallucinatory quality of slow motion—which rhymes perfectly with the dance and trance possession she is filming—and its ability to let us see details we would otherwise miss in the frenetic action.]

Deep Hearts is a dream of the Garawal ceremony, stolen from the sleep of an anthropologist; the woozy memory of events one has witnessed in eight days of desert sun. As science, it is probably as accurate a description as a more linear recreation. But, unlike science, it leaves its enigmas unsolved. Its last lines of narration are among the most abstract in the genre:

> The visitors leave as suddenly as they appeared, and, with the diminishing rains, they will resume their nomadic lives. They go knowing what they would hope to be, an ideal example having been selected from their midst. But this may only serve to remind them of the desires that cannot be met, and which, with the uncertainty of whether choices are really theirs, still lie at the bottom of their deep hearts.

This dream, then, becomes an expression of unfulfilled desire in an unstable society. It is interesting that we barely glimpse, and only from afar, the winner of the contest: this is a study of longing, not achievement. And, uniquely in ethnographic film— which seems to cover everything except what people really think about (other than money)—*Deep Hearts* is a study of erotic longing: the young women posed in tableaux of virginal meekness facing the men (we watch the dancers over the shoulder of one of them); the auto-eroticism of these dancing men dressed as women; the old women who, no longer in the courtship game, must ritually insult them; and the old men who, from the image of their past selves, select the most beautiful.

The film underscores what is obvious elsewhere: there are vast areas of human life to which scientific methodology is inapt; to which ethnographic description must give way to the ethnopoetic: a series of concrete and luminous images, arranged by intuition rather than prescription, and whose shifting configurations—like the points of and between the constellations—map out a piece of a world.

Simultaneous time, the babble of voices overlapping and interrupting each other, the rapid succession of images, the cacophony of programmed and random sounds: all modern art is urban art, and all film—being born with this century—is an image of the city. What then does one do with the subjects of ethnography who, with few exceptions, lead rural lives? The anthropological monograph is, as James Clifford has pointed out, this century's version of the pastoral, and its writing can and does draw on its literary antecedents. Film, however, with its short takes, shifting camera angles, and multiple viewpoints, is as intrinsically anti-pastoral as its filmmakers themselves. To take it (and oneself) into the countryside of the tribe, one may either deny its (and one's own) nature—as most ethnographic filmmakers have done—or somehow discover a way into one's subject.

With *Forest of Bliss,* Robert Gardner has taken his modernist sensibility into an urban setting, however, one that is uniquely archaic. The result is a panoramic "city" film in the tradition that begins with Paul Strand and Charles Sheeler's *Mannahatta* (1921) and Walther Ruttmann's *Berlin: Symphony of the City* (1927), and whose latest incarnation is the first half of Wim Wender's *Wings of Desire* (1987). And yet the nature of his subject, Benares, India, cannot help but insert the film into myth.

Benares is at least three thousand years old, and the oldest continually inhabited city on earth. Moreover, it always has had the same primary function, as the place where each day the countless dead are burned or dropped into the Ganges, and the living purified. To visit the sacred zones of the city, along the river, is like finding priests of Isis still practicing in Luxor. No other living city exists so purely in mythic time.

Similarly, the city itself is an iconographic representation of the passage from this world to the next: a labyrinth of bazaars, temples, and houses for the dying opens out onto steps that lead down to the river (at one section of steps the dead are burned); the wide river itself, cleansing all, and beyond, distantly visible, the other shore.

These are universally recognizable symbols, from which—with a host of others: the kite perched between heaven and earth, the scavenging dogs, the boats that carry the dead to the other side, the purifying fire, the flowers of veneration—Gardner has constructed a montage of the eternally repeatable. It is both a study of the mechanics of death (the organization of Benares' cremation industry) and a map of the Hindu cosmology of death— almost entirely presented through iconic images. It is surely the most tightly edited film in the genre, truly a fugue of reiterated elements, and one whose astonishing use of sound sustains the cyclical structure by carrying over the natural sounds of one scene into the next—Godard's technique adapted to a completely different purpose.

Most radically, Gardner has eliminated all verbal explanations. There is no narration, the dialogue is not subtitled, and there is only one intertitle, a single line from the Yeats translation of the Upanishads. *Forest of Bliss,* more than any other film, reinforces the outsider status of both the filmmaker and the viewer: we must look, listen, remain alert, accept confusion, draw our own tentative conclusions, find parallels from within our own experiences. Travelers confronting the exotic, we are also the living standing before the dead.

Needless to say, the film has driven the scientists mad. The newsletter of the Society of Visual Anthropologists ran a series of polemics against it, filled with lines like "Technology has left pure imagery behind, and anthropologists ought to do so too." (The same writer commenting that, given the sanitary problems of disposing corpses in the river, an interview with a public health official would have been informative.)

These are the people who prefer a kinship chart to *Anna Karenina,* but their project is intrinsically doomed: only elaborated metaphor and complex aesthetic structures are capable of even beginning to represent human nature and events: configurations of pure imagery will always leave technology behind.

Nearly all ethnographic filmmakers, in interviews, have remarked that the genre is, so many decades later, still in its infancy. It is difficult to disagree. The latest films selected for a recent Margaret Mead Film Festival in New York were generally more of the same: Every film had a narrator, many of them still speaking to a room full of slow children: "This is rice cooking. Rice is grown in their fields." Films still open with lines like, "This is the heart of Africa." There are still moments of incredible chauvinism, as when a narrator explains, "These village children have few toys, yet they are happy," or when, in a British film on the huge Kumbh Mela festival in India, the spiritual leaders of various temples are called bishops, abbots, and deacons, as though this were a tea party in Canterbury. Sixty years after *Nanook,* families were still pretending to sleep before the cameras.

A few things had changed: thanks to new high-speed films, many featured extraordinary night scenes, lit only by fires or candles. The effects of the West are no longer kept hidden: in one scene, a shaman in a trance stopped chanting to change the cassette in his tape recorder; and it was remarkable how many of the people, from scattered corners of the world, were wearing the same T-shirts with goofy slogans in English. Nearly every film featured synch sound and subtitled dialogue; the films were full of local speech.

It is impossible to separate what may be the next stage of ethnographic film from the fate of its subjects: extinction for some and tremendous cultural change for the rest. But there was an instant in a recent film, Howard Reid's *The Shaman and His Apprentice* (1989), that was, for me, a sudden glimpse into how much has been missing in the genre, and what its future may bring: when film technology is no longer a Western domain; when the observed become the observers; when ethnography becomes a communal self-portraiture, as complex as any representation of *us;* when the erotic can enter in as expression, not voyeurism; when *they,* at last, do all the talking.

The film follows a healer named José, of the Yamunawa people of the Peruvian Amazon, as he educates and initiates a young disciple, Caraca. In one scene José takes Caraca for his first visit to the nearest large town. The trip has only one purpose: to go to the local movie house, where there is an important lesson about healing to be learned:

"Cinema," José explains, "is exactly like the visions sick people have when they are dying."

[1990]

THE CITY OF PEACE

When they seized power in the year 750, the House of Abbasid, descendants of the Prophet's uncle, acquired an empire of distant reach from India to the Atlantic coast of Europe. Twelve years later, on a day fixed by a Persian astrologer for the prominence of Jupiter, work began on their new capital, Madinat as-Salam, the City of Peace. As center of the empire and image of the world, the city was built in the form of a circle divided by a cross; its four gates the four directions to the four corners of the earth.

For 500 years, though the edges of the empire eroded and broke off, the city—still known by the name of the village it had replaced, Baghdad—luxuriated. The most cosmopolitan city in the world of that time, with ships docked—there at the confluence of the Euphrates and Tigris—from China, India, Russia, Spain, the North and Black African kingdoms; with its schools of painting, poetry, philosophy, astronomy, philology, mathematics; its translations of the Greek texts that would ultimately impel the European Renaissance; where fortunes could be quickly made and even more quickly spent. (Sinbad, for one, became a sailor because he had dissipated an enormous inheritance on evening entertainment and "costly robes.") Perennial symbol of the metropolis as pleasure palace: I write from a city once known, not so long ago, as Baghdad on the Hudson.

The poets of that city—particularly in its first 300 years—were noted for their rejection of traditional verse forms, their unembarrassed hedonism in many varieties, their scorn for religious and social orthodoxies, their sycophancy in court and their bitter polemics outside it, their elaborate prosodic techniques and increasingly pedantic literary criticism. Their form of choice was the *qit'a*, literally a "fragment"—not so much a modernist shard from a vanished whole as an arrow of light in the gloom, a twinge

160

of perfection, as in the famous couplet (an entire poem) by the 8th-century poet Abbas Ibn al-Ahnaf:

> When she walks with her girl servants
> Her beauty is a moon between swaying lanterns[1]

The misanthropic, anti-clerical, skeptical, metaphysical, blind anchorite poet Abu al-Ala al-Ma'arri (973–1052) is generally considered to be their greatest. Among his works is a parody of the Quran, for which he was criticized, but not condemned. It is said that Dante read him in translation, and one could easily mistake the couplet that closes this poem by Ma'arri as yet one more eerie and exact image from the *Commedia:*

> Each sunset warns quiet men who look ahead
> That light will end; and each day postman Death
>
> Knocks on our door. Although he does not speak,
> He hands us a standing invitation.
>
> Be like those skeleton horses which scent battle
> And fear to eat. They wait chewing their bridles.

Ma'arri wrote:

> Some people are like an open grave:
> You give it the thing you love most
> And get nothing in return.

And, a thousand years ago in Baghdad, he wrote a line that, in New York in late January 1991—days filled with fabricated images of the barbarity of the new enemy we were slaughtering—made me, if only for a few hours, turn off the television:

> Don't let your life be governed by what disturbs you.

[1991]

[1] The translations here are by Abdullah al-Udhari and George Wightman, from their *Birds through a Ceiling of Alabaster* (Penguin, 1975).

A Clarion for the Quincentenary

In November 1620, the *Mayflower* is anchored in the shallows off the coast of Cape Cod. The men, terrified of what one of them calls the "hideous & desolate wilderness, full of wild beasts & wild men," must wade nearly three-fourths of a mile through freezing water to reach shore. There, they report back, all is surprisingly calm: no people. The next day is the Sabbath and they pray. The following day the women come ashore to do the washing, and all of the company gorge themselves on quahogs, cherrystones, and mussels, which make them sick.

Two days later, a small party led by their chief of security, Myles Standish, sets out to explore. They come across a group of six men, who dart into the woods. Pursuing them, the expedition, with their heavy arms, becomes entangled in the thick brush. At last they come out in a clearing: a field of corn. There are freshly made mounds which they uncover. Some are graves; others are granaries, with baskets full of yellow, red, and blue maize stored for the winter. Thanking God for His bounty, they steal the corn.

Having repaired a shallop to carry them along the coast in search of a river they think they've seen, and a possible site for settlement, a larger party pushes off in a snowstorm ten days later. They first return to the place they've named Corn Hill. To loot the mounds again they must break the frozen ground with their cutlasses. They find more corn, a bag of beans, a gourd containing oil.

They discover two round houses, evidently abandoned at their approach. Inside are various mats; wooden bowls, trays, and dishes; clay pots; large baskets ingeniously made of crab shells; woven baskets, some of them "curiously wrought with black and white in pretty works"; deer heads, freshly killed; antlers and deer feet and eagle claws; baskets of dried acorns; a piece of broiled herring; tobacco seed; and "sundry bundles" of dried flowers and sedge and bulrushes. They take the "best things" away with them, but decide to leave "the houses standing," as their diarist reports.

Wandering in the snow, in the empty stretches of an un-colonized America, they come across a mound, covered with boards, that is longer and larger than the others they've seen. They dig, and find a mat, and under it a bow. Then another mat, and under that, a board two feet long and "finely carved and painted, with three tines or broaches on the top, like a crown." Then bowls and trays, dishes and trinkets. Another mat, and under that, two sacks, one large, one small. The larger is filled with a fine red powder, and the partially consumed flesh, bones, and skull of a man. The man has long blonde hair. Alongside him is a knife, a pack needle, and "two or three old iron things," wrapped in a sailor's canvas cassock and a pair of cloth breeches. They open the smaller sack and find the same red powder, and the head and bones of a small child. On his or her legs and arms are bracelets of fine white beads. Beside the child is a tiny bow. Standish and the men take some of the "prettiest things," cover up the grave, and move on. A month later they have found their place in Plymouth.

Who is this sailor? The Pilgrims were the first white settlers, but there had been occasional English and Breton fishermen along the coast for some years. Champlain had explored the area in 1605. Captain John Smith of the Virginia colonies had come in 1614, stolen canoes from the Indians and traded them back for beaver skins, and drawn a detailed map. In 1616 or 1617 a French ship had been wrecked in a local storm. By the time the Pilgrims arrived, it is estimated that 95,000 of the 100,000 Indians in the area had already died of the newly imported diseases.

And this child? Indian, white, or both? The sailor's child, a coincidental death, a victim? Did they die together, or was the child killed to join the sailor in the other world? Only one thing is certain: both were buried by the Indians, and with honor.

Standish and the sailor: one alive in history, in a linear time that is all future; the other dead in myth, in a cycle of time that has ended abruptly and forever, for him and for a world. At the founding of the New England, this impossibly chance encounter: a point of origin where the road splits into what America did and did not become.

Myles Standish, not a Separatist like the Pilgrims but a Roman Catholic of aristocratic background, a Standish of Standish, who was defrauded of his inheritance and became a mercenary in the Low Countries. The Pilgrims hired him as a military adviser, a bodyguard for the landing. He was one of the few to survive the first winter at Plymouth; he built the fort and oversaw what was for decades the most secure English colony in America. He was sent to England to negotiate the complicated property rights for the colonists, who were supposed to be in Virginia. And he was sent to Merry Mount to destroy the orgiastic colony led by Thomas Morton, where drunken Indian men traded pelts for guns, while drunken white men and Indian "lasses in beaver coats" danced around the Maypole.

Standish who kills for money, who builds the fortress to keep us in and them without, who steals their food and trinkets and—through Samoset and Squanto—their savvy, the businessman who gets laws changed to his advantage and the cop who enforces them, who treats the dead with disdain, who brings order to wilderness and wildness, the true Separatist, the founding father.

Standish standing over the found father, this sailor who crossed over. White skin and red skin, red powder and white beads, iron knife and wooden bow, man and, in death, woman, a dead Madonna with dead child, fair-haired god and goddess of the fair-haired corn nearby.

And the child, symbol of a blending, a future generation that will generally not occur in North America. In his place, the day before his grave is opened, another child is born, the first in the New England colonies. He is named Peregrine (pilgrim and bird of prey) White.

And the *Mayflower,* on its next voyage, sailing to Africa to pick up slaves.

And Plymouth Rock, today in the newspapers—"defaced" they say, but "signed" is more accurate—with a huge red swastika. A swastika whose author, in his ignorance, has drawn backwards. Intended clarion for racial purity, for a Pilgrim and Puritan land, it is instead a revenging light: the ancient American Indian symbol for the sun.

[August 1991]

DREAMS FROM THE HOLOTHURIANS

The ocean covers 73% of the earth's surface and over 80% of this surface is a soft-sediment-covered sea floor. This is the home of the abyssal holothurians. These animals are the most evident organisms seen in abyssal photographs, and the combination of these circumstances leads one to the inescapable conclusion that holothurians are the dominant large animals of the major part of the earth's surface. Holothurians feeding on bottom sediments mix and till the surface mud on an enormous scale, producing features more widespread and more visibly evident than those produced by any other animal on earth.

Two globe-headed divers walk on the ocean floor, attached by rubber hoses to their mother-ship, a small but luxuriously appointed submarine. Though tens of thousands of fathoms down, the scene is bright with the reddish glow of burning lava from an undersea volcano:

There indeed before my eyes, ruined, destroyed, lay a town, its roof open to the sky, its temples fallen, its arches dislocated, its columns lying on the ground, from which one could still recognize the massive character of Tuscan architecture. Further on, some remains of a giant aqueduct; here the high base of an Acropolis, with the floating outline of a Parthenon; there traces of a quay, as if an ancient port had formerly abutted on the borders of the ocean, and disappeared with its merchant vessels and its war-galleys. Further on again, long lines of sunken walls and broad, deserted streets—a perfect Pompeii escaped beneath the waters. Such was the sight that Captain Nemo brought before my eyes!

Where was I? Where was I? I must know at any cost. I tried to speak, but Captain Nemo stopped me with a gesture, and picking up a piece of chalkstone, advanced to a rock of black basalt, and traced the one word:

ATLANTIS

Atlantis!

Why did the Hebrews, Aztecs, Chaldeans, Arameans, Maya, Hindus, Toltecs, Zoroastrians, Chippewas, Greeks, and Delawares all have myths of a great flood?

Why did both the Egyptians and the Mesoamericans build pyramids?

Why did the Egyptians, the Inca, and the Maya all employ the arch?

Why did the Mexicans believe their culture-hero Quetzalcoatl came from the East? And why is he depicted with a beard?

Atlantis! Herodotus tells of a people in the west, the Atarantes, who have no names for individuals, and who curse the sun at noon for its heat. And west of them are the Atlantes, named for Mt. Atlas, which they call the Pillar of Heaven and whose peak is permanently hidden in the clouds. A people who eat no living thing, and never dream.

Why did the Egyptians, the Guanches of the Canaries, and the Peruvians all mummify their dead?

Why did the Aztecs believe that they originally came from a place called *Aztlan*?

Where did the Phoenicians get their alphabet?

Why did the Egyptians paint themselves as red men?

Who were the Aryans?

Atlantis! Plato hears Socrates tell of a story passed down through generations from Solon, who heard it from Egyptian priests. That beyond the Pillars of Hercules there was an island larger than Libya and Asia put together; that it was the way to other islands, and beyond them another continent; that it was rich in fruits, elephants, and the mysterious gleaming red mineral *orichalc*. An island ruled by Poseidon, who had five sets of male twins and divided the kingdom among them, naming the land after the eldest, Atlas. That nine thousand years ago, Atlantis, having conquered Egypt and half of Italy, waged war on Athens—that is, the original, lost city of Athens—and was defeated. That this once divine race, who had cared nothing for wealth, had become more human and "unseemly." That Zeus had decided to punish them with earthquakes and a flood that destroyed both Atlantis and most of the land of the virtuous Platonic republic of Athens, which had never recovered.

Where was the Garden of Eden, Asgard, Mt. Olympus, the Elysian Fields?

How did the Bronze Age come to Europe without an Age of Copper?

Why is Poseidon, a god of the sea, depicted as driving a chariot drawn by horses?

Why did the medieval monk Cosmos place "the Land where men dwelt before the Flood" on the left side of his map?

What is the origin of the word *Atlantic*? Why is the range in northwest Africa called the *Atlas* mountains?

Why does *atl* mean "water" in the Aztec language?

Why did the Egyptians believe that the underworld was in the West?

Atlantis! Theopompos writes of an Outer Continent, inhabited by people twice our size, and their country called No Return, forever shrouded in red mist, with two rivers, Pleasure and Grief. A land whose giants had come east to pillage, and had found nothing in the Known World worth stealing.

Atlantis! Aristotle says Plato made it up. Amelius says he was talking metaphorically about the stars. Diogenes Laertius says it was merely an ethical dialogue. Iamblichos and Syrianos say it's both true and an allegory. Origenes Adamantius, Numenius, and Porphyrios say it's only an allegory. Arnobius Afer, Krantor, Philo Judaeus, Poseidonios, and Tertullian believe him. Plutarch, Strabo, and Pliny the Elder say it's doubtful.

Why did the Egyptians erect obelisks inscribed with hieroglyphs and the Mesoamericans erect stelae inscribed with hieroglyphs?

Why did both the ancient Europeans and the ancient Americans bury their dead under mounds? And why did they all bury food, weapons, clothes, and trinkets with them?

Why did both the Egyptians and the Peruvians have the plow?

Why is the Aztec flood-survivor named *Nata,* which is almost *Noah?*

Why did the Mandan Indians have blue eyes and venerate an ark called the Big Canoe? And why did they tell the myth of a single white man escaping the great waters?

Francisco López de Gómara found it in America—in 1553 he was the first—and John Dee and Alexander von Humboldt were among his many followers. In 1570 Jean de Serre, known as Serranus, found it in Palestine.

Atlantis! Sir Francis Bacon tells the tale of a ship, blown off course from Peru to China, that lands in Bensalem, founded by refugees from the lost continent. It is a Christian constitutional monarchy, devoted to philosophy and scientific research, which by 1626 had already invented airplanes, submarines, and air-conditioning.

Olaüs Rudbeck, a 17th-century Swede, studied the *Edda* and found it, and the origin of all European and Asian peoples, in Sweden. A century later Jean Bailly found it first in Mongolia and then in the sea off Spitsbergen, and tried to convince Voltaire.

Why does the Roman god Jove hold thunderbolts in his hand and the Mexican god of thunder, Mixcoatl, hold a bundle of arrows?

Why does the Quran speak of the people of *Ad,* who built the City of Pillars and were destroyed for their wickedness?

Why did the Scythians and the Maya elongate the heads of their babies? And why were the Pharaohs bald with flat foreheads?

Who were *Ad*am, *Ad*onis, the Persian god Mashab-*ad,* and the Hindu gods the *Ad*itya?

Why do Norwegian lemmings swim out to sea, as though looking for a land that is no longer there, circle aimlessly, and die?

Hafer, an 18th-century Prussian with no first name, found it in Prussia. Francis Wilford, a British officer in India, found it in 1805 off the coast of England, where the events in the Old Testament had taken place, and his theories were picked up by William Blake:

> On those vast shady hills between America and
>   Albion's shore,
> Now barr'd out by the Atlantic sea, call'd Atlantean
>   hills,
> Because from their bright summits you may pass to
>   the Golden world,
> An ancient palace, archetype of mighty Emperies,
> Rears its immortal pinnacles, built in the forest of
>   God
> By Ariston, the king of beauty, for his stolen bride.

Atlantis!

> In one night the Atlantic Continent was caught up
>   with the Moon
> And became an Opake Globe, far distant, clad with
>   moony beams.

Why did the Assyrians carve reliefs of pineapples?

Why are there crosses in all world religions?

Why did the Hindus have a fish-god?

Why did both the Egyptians and the Peruvians take a census of their people?

Why did the ancient Irish have tobacco pipes?

Why are both the Germans and the American Indians scared of wolves?

Atlantis! John Ruskin harangues a group of businessmen in

Bradford: Their temples of gold, their wasting of the country-side, their exploitation of the workers will lead to a calamity like the one the Atlanteans brought upon themselves.

Atlantis! The Catalan Jacinto Verdaguer, chaplain to the Compania Transatlantica, Spiritual Counselor to the Marqués de Comillas in Havana, writes a Christian classical nationalist epic: *L'Atlantida.* God punishes Atlantis for its greed, sparing only the virtuous lands of Spain. All of the Atlantean treasures are moved to Iberia, which becomes the Elysian Fields, the source of the Golden Fleece, and all the promised lands of the Egyptians, Hebrews, and Greeks. Even the golden orange tree from the Garden of the Hesperides is planted by Hercules in Cadíz. [Though next to it, this being Spain, grows a mysterious deformed tree dripping blood: tears for the Atlantean dead.] Hercules splits the mountains of Atlantis in two, to become the Pillars, and the Mediterranean Sea rushes over the land. He inscribes the words NON PLUS ULTRA on the rock of Gibraltar: no one may venture beyond until peace and purity reign. Cut: to Columbus and a crew of united Spaniards—Andalucians, Galicians, Catalans, Castilians, and Cantabrians—on their way to the new Atlantis, gathered on deck to pray for safe passage.

Why, nearly everywhere, is gold associated with the sun, and silver with the moon?

Why did the American Indians and the ancient Europeans believe in ghosts?

Why did both worlds like to drink fermented intoxicating beverages? And why did both use scales and weights and mirrors?

Why did the American Indians and the ancient Celts draw spirals?

Why did both the Greeks and the people of the Amazon have poison-tipped arrows?

Why did William Penn claim that the Indians of Pennsylvania look like Jews?

Félix Berlioux found it in 1874 near Casablanca, and inspired

Pierre Benoit's *L'Atlantide*, the tale of Queen Antinéa with her pet leopard on a leash—filmed by Pabst and Ulmer, and once played by María Montez—whose abandoned lovers, with nothing else to live for, commit suicide and are placed in a vast and crowded crypt.

Atlantis! Its greatest scholar, Ignatius T. T. Donnelly (1831–1901), was Lieutenant Governor of Minnesota, Congressman for eight years, twice a candidate for Vice President, and wrote a prophetic novel of the coming century that sold a million copies. In other books he proved that the Ice Age was caused by a collision of the earth and a comet, and that Sir Francis Bacon wrote all of Shakespeare's plays. His masterwork, *The Antediluvian World* (1882), amasses incredible evidence to show that Atlantis was the source of world civilization; that Europe and the Americas were Atlantean colonies, and Egypt the original outpost; that the kings, queens, and heroes of Atlantis became the gods and goddesses of world mythology; that the Egyptian and the Peruvian versions were the remnants of the true religion of Atlantis; that the Bronze Age and the alphabet were invented there; and that survivors of the catastrophe spread the tales that became the world myths of the Deluge.

How did Plato know about coconuts?

Why do the Hindus refer to illusion as *Maya*?

Why were animals worshiped in both the New World and the Old? And why did both use dreams for prophesying?

Why does Homer mention an ancient race of navigators named the *Cares*, which is almost *Caribs*?

Why are there three Armenian cities cited by Ptolemy as *Chol, Colua*, and *Cholima*, and three Mexican cities named *Cholula, Coluacan*, and *Colima*?

Why is "me" *me* in Mandan and *mi*, pronounced "me," in Welsh?

Atlantis! Augustus Le Plongeon, the first to excavate the Maya ruins in the Yucatán, deciphers the glyphs and discovers that they tell the story of the princes Coh and Aac, rivals for the hand of their sister Moo, Queen of Atlantis. Coh is accepted, but is murdered by Aac, whose armies overrun Atlantis as the continent begins to sink. Moo flees to Egypt, where she builds the Sphinx as a monument to her husband/brother, changes her name to Isis, and is the founder of Egyptian civilization. The Greek alphabet, recited in the proper order, is actually a Mayan poem on the fate of Moo.

Why did the American Indians, the Romans, and the Chinese venerate their ancestors?

Why did the Phoenicians have an evil spirit named *Zebub,* and the Peruvians an evil spirit named *Cupay,* which sounds different but is in fact the same name?

Why is Quechua so similar to Arabic?

If the Azores are named after *azores,* hawks, then how did the rabbits and mice that hawks eat reach those islands?

Why does Savonarola in his famous portrait look like Sitting Bull?

Atlantis! In India Madame Blavatsky goes into a trance and receives a palm-leaf book: The *Book of Dzyan,* written in Atlantis in the ancient Senzar language: "The last Vibration of the Seventh Eternity thrills through Infinitude. The Mother swells, expanding from without like the Bud of the Lotus . . . After great throes she cast out her old Three and put on her new Seven Skins, and stood in her First One." There are seven Rounds of Life, and seven Root Races, and seven Sub-Races: astral jellyfish in the Imperishable Sacred Land, and egg-laying hermaphroditic Lemurians with four arms, and Atlanteans of course, and the race that lives under the North Pole.

Lost! Plutarch claimed that Solon began an epic poem on Atlantis, and gave it up. Lost! Plato's account of the continent, *Critias,* ends suddenly in mid-sentence: "And when he had called them together, he spoke as follows:"

Leo Frobenius, the African scholar championed by Pound, found it in Nigeria, along with the city of Tarshish, where Jonah was headed. All civilization, he wrote, had traveled west from a genuinely lost continent in the Pacific; reports of the Yorubas (who were thought to be the Atlanteans) had confused them with their Pacific ancestors.

Why did both Roman and Iroquois couples share a piece of food as part of their wedding ceremony?

Why is the Mayan word *hurakan*, god of the storm, so similar to the old Swedish *hurra*, meaning "to be driven along," to *hurry?*

Why did both the Jews and the Mexicans offer water to strangers to wash their feet?

Why did the Maya have a city called *Mayapan*, which is a combination of *Maya* and the Greek god *Pan?*

Why did the Aztecs have an elective monarchy like 19th-century Poland?

Why do the Basques speak Algonquin?

Atlantis! Heinrich Schliemann's grandson Paul claims that he inherited a letter, an envelope, and an owl-headed vase of unknown provenance. The letter instructed that only a family member willing to devote his life to the material contained in the envelope and vase should open them. He pledged his life, and broke the vase. Inside were four square coins and a metal plaque inscribed in Phoenician, *Issued in the Temple of Transparent Walls.* He opened the envelope, and found his grandfather's secret notes from the excavation of Troy: the finding of a bronze urn full of coins marked *From the King Cronos of Atlantis.* Young Schliemann then set off for Tibet, where he discovered a Chaldean account of the destruction of the Land of the Seven Cities. Schliemann reports his findings to the *New York American* in 1912, promising to reveal much more in a forthcoming book.

Lost! Sir Francis Bacon never finished *The New Atlantis.*

Paul Borchardt found it in the swamps of Shott el Jerid in Tunisia. Albert Herrmann, a Frisian, found it Friesland. Victor Bérard found it in Carthage. Ellen Whishaw, director of the

Anglo-Spanish-American School of Archeology, found an Atlantean outpost in Seville. Count Byron Khun de Prorok found the tomb of its Queen in the Ahaggar Mountains, and claimed the Tuaregs as direct descendants.

Lost! William Emmette Coleman, a disgruntled acolyte, decided to devote himself to exposing Madame Blavatsky's plagiarisms in the *Book of Dzyan* from ancient Indian texts. But his library and notes were destroyed in the San Francisco earthquake, and he died soon after.

Atlantis! becomes Otlontis which becomes Oluntos which becomes Olumpus, which is Olympus.

Lost! After his newspaper article, Paul Schliemann was never heard from again, his book never published, and the Schliemann family claimed they had no one named Paul.

Atlantis! Rudolf Steiner writes how the Atlanteans had no ability to reason, but that they had trained themselves in the mnemonic arts, and could even pass on their collected memories to their children. When faced with a problem, they found the solution from precedence; but if it was a new problem, they could only experiment blindly. They used words to heal wounds immediately, and flew in aircraft that ran on "life force."

Atlantis! Lewis Spence in 1924 solves the chronological discrepancies between its destruction and the rise of the Mexican and Peruvian civilizations. The earthquake had split the lost continent in two: the eastern island of Atlantis and the western island of Antilia, which was preserved in memory as the Antilles. The Atlanteans invaded Europe, and then thousands of years later, with the destruction of both continents, the Antilians escaped to the Americas.

Lost! The retired British officer Lieutenant Colonel Percy H. Fawcett went looking for it in the Amazon in 1925 and never returned. Lost! The French gold prospector Apollinaire Frot returned from those same jungles announcing archeological discoveries of such magnitude that he feared the consequences of revealing them, and died soon after.

F. Gidon found it off the coast of Brittany, and declared it French. The Englishman W. C. Beaumont found it in England, "birthplace of all civilization," and proved that the Pillars of Hercules were the English Channel and that Plato's Athens was in Scotland. He synthesized his findings in his lifework, *Britain: The Key to World History.*

Atlantis! In 1929 the backwoods psychic Edgar Cayce predicts its reappearance in 1968. In 1968 massive stone walls are discovered under the waters off Bimini in the Bahamas.

Lost! Manuel de Falla and José María Sert collaborated on a "scenic cantata," *Atlántida,* based on the Verdaguer epic. But Sert died, and then de Falla died, the piece unfinished after eighteen years of work.

John Michell found its remains in the global energy lines of Avebury, Carnac, Giza, Nazca, and the whole of China south of the Great Wall, which was "formed to a single design." Charles Berlitz found that it is still there, in the Bermuda Triangle, luring ships down. Erik von Däniken found it in outer space, the planet Atlantis whose spaceship pioneers had first colonized the earth.

Lost Atlantis! It was all a dream from the holothurians. The holothurians, despised by men, called "sea cucumbers" after that insipid vegetable, dismissed as cylindrical purplish blobs, nothing more than a mouth and an anus, forever filtering mud in the gloom of the ocean floor—it was the holothurians who did it. For each is the cell of a huge collective brain, a brain trapped in millions of useless bodies that inhabit the dullest stretches on earth.

So, to amuse itself, this brain has spun stories along its submarine network, stories that bubbled up and randomly entered the dreams of the sleeping people above. Stories that provoked strange longings for the ocean floor: that the origin of all life began there, that forgotten kingdoms lie there in the mud, along with the shipwrecks of fantastic wealth. A dream that Solon and Plato and Bacon and de Falla and the others could only partially remember: they wrote it down, then went to sleep again to recover the rest, and never could. A dream that has led so many to dive into the sea and keep swimming down.

Atlantis! In the dark the holothurians eat and excrete and move on and eat, inching forward, thinking, sending out their mental flares in the hope that someone, something, anything will drop by and relieve the tedium of their biological fate, down there, at the bottom of the sea, with the calcified sponges, magnesium nodules, the crushed spines of sea urchins, the ghosts of coelenterates, unexploded torpedoes, skeletons of bathypterids and halosaurs, the hieroglyphic tracks of sea pens and ophiuroids, fecal coils, the waving arms of a burrowed brittle-star, manganese-encrusted dolphin teeth, the remains of a jettisoned crate of manilla-envelope clasps, zeolite crystals, pillows of basalt, calcareous shells of pteropods, the sinister egg-casings of skates, the broken anti-matter locks from a crashed spaceship, the short-crested ripples of sand, and the scour moats forming in globigerina ooze.

[1991]

New Directions Paperbooks — A Partial Listing

For complete listing request free catalog from
New Directions, 80 Eighth Avenue, New York 10011

†Bilingual

7/18/94

PS
3573
E3928
O98
1992

For complete listing request free catalog from
New Directions, 80 Eighth Avenue, New York 10011

†Bilingu

OUTSIDE STORIES

Essays by Eliot Weinberger

Unpredictable and uncanonical, Eliot Weinberger's essays are the "outside stories" of cultural migrations. The fifteen pieces collected here range from the history of the Salman Rushdie affair to the dream of Atlantis, from the turf wars among ethnographic filmmakers to the unlikely romance between poetry and espionage, from the pilgrims in Plymouth to the students in Tiananmen Square. Above all, Weinberger's concern is poetry—whether written in medieval Baghdad or by Mexicans in Japan—and the perennially underground yet global network through which it travels. With his modernist sensibility and internationalist perspective, Weinberger's inventive prose transports old myths and texts to the strange realities of contemporary life. Eliot Weinberger is the author, translator, and editor of over fifteen books, among them *The Collected Poems of Octavio Paz* (1987) and his previous book of essays, *Works on Paper* (1986). He is the winner of PEN's 1992 Gregory Kolovakos Prize, for the promotion of Hispanic literature in English translation.

"One would love, someday, to have the equivalent [of Eliot Weinberger] in France."—*Action Poétique* (Paris)

"The translator of Octavio Paz is also a literary essayist of the highest order."—*ALA Booklist*

"Weinberger's perspective is shrewd and iconoclastic, his writing is passionate and clear, and the questions he raises merit attention from the less word-bound as well as the literary among us."—Nan Levinson, *Boston Review*

Cover Photograph by Henri Cartier-Bresson (Magnum Photos, Inc.); design by Hermann Strohbach

A NEW DIRECTIONS
PAPERBOOK
NDP751

USA $10.95
CAN $13.99

ISBN 0-8112-1221-1